DAMNATION
BENEATH THE
FROZEN APOCALYPSE

FOR

By The Grim Reverend Steven Rage

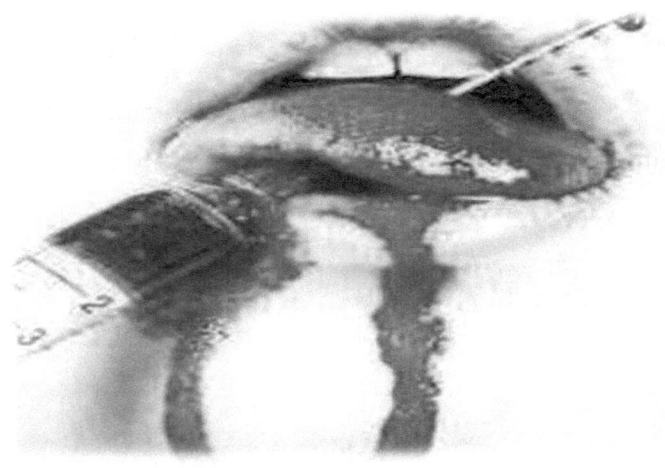

Morbidbooks Is A Grotesque Bizarro Ballet Where The Most Profane Things Occur. An Impious And Perverse Dwelling Of Dark Revulsion. A Cozy Cottage Where Torture Porn And Brutal Bible Tales Are Devised. A Quiet Place To Relax And Spin Tales Of Depravity And Wickedness. A Halfway House For The Disturbed Where Rules No Longer Apply. A Safe Haven For Deviant Serial Killers To Hatch Their Wretched Schemes. Bring Your Pets. The Tasty Ones Are Always Welcome.

HTTPS://WWW.MORBIDBOOKS.WORDPRESS.COM

BAD NOTION TRAVELING POTION

"I beheld the wretch, the miserable monster whom I had created."

Victor Frankenstein

–MARY W. SHELLEY

PRO TERMINUS

WE REMEMBER SO CLEARLY HIS BODY FLUIDS. As We stared, enraptured, they dripped down nicely into the collection pan. The big commercial fish dehydrator was leaching out every tiny liquid jeweled drop of Elron Hunt. We watched it drip, transfixed by its drop by drop progression. We waited patiently for the pan to fill.

We had already selected a large soup bowl and equally spacious spoon. Elron moved slightly, startling us out of our revelry. We rose out of our chair and made sure that his airway was open and secure and that Uncle was still breathing; for just a little while longer, anyway. Then it will no longer matter. No, Sir; not one tiny bit. Then he cannot be. Elron Hunt does not need to live forever. No one does. No one except for Us, that is. We also had a clear line tubing of icy water trickling down his gullet. The extra fluid infused will aid to force more of Us out of him, and retrieve some more of ourselves. Eventually, We will be made whole for the very first time in our collective experience. In a sense, We shall be born anew.

Elron Hunt opened his eyes and he stared, helpless, at his own ceiling. We added a minute dollop of Downtown Leroy Brown into his line of water. His eyes soon clouded over as he turned his head and tried to focus in on Us. The uncertainty stamped on his face was a bit distressing. Elron recognized the meat puppet We were using, but he did not know Us. We were way too deep down for that. As the pan filled, the thick wool of darkness was pulled over his eyes, allowing Elron to die rather peacefully and in his sleep. We need to reclaim from him, but We're trying to be nice about it. A part of him, We could tell, wants this. Even if he doesn't know who or what We are exactly, he wants to let Us go.

There is no reason for Elron Hunt to suffer. He has to die so We can grow and become, but We don't have to be a huge Richard about it. Going to the Next serenely is just fine by Us.

We went back to our chair, tableside. The collection tray was flush. We tipped the tray into our bowl, slap-sloshing lumps like a loose stool. It was cooling down to a nice, warm body temperature. We spoon it up and savor the salty goodness. The bloody lumps were first-rate and substantive. We squashed the lumps between our tongue and the roof of our mouth. They explode with flavor like the greased juices of cooked burger meat. We can sense some of our presence; maybe even touch a taste of Us as well. The compulsion to rejoin is instinctive and intense. We can already feel, as We scoop and swallow, scoop and swallow, ourselves thickening and gaining substance. We were attracting and accepting our lost essence. We're manifesting this, our coalescence.

We finished the bowl, feeling better already. We wait for more. And when the fluids of Elron Hunt are completely consumed, We still have the jerked meat to work through. That will take some time. The fluids and bits are gobbled directly, but our puppet can only consume so much meat a day. We also have to get him to skin the carcass, do something with the bones...

Elron Hunt's fluids resumed exodus. We have to wait for the collection pan to refill, before We can eat some more of ourselves. We will become whole. We can feel it. It will plainly take more time and labor. And more people.

We shall go backwards...

UNUS

THE GOOD DOCTOR STEPPED OUT OF THE TELEPORTER and into his office. He was below ground, in a sub-basement level of Hell's Mouth Determining Hospital. The Good Doctor held his large coffee and his newspaper, and he had his over-sized travel slippers on. He went to his spacious desk and laid the items down on its face. He turned to the closet behind the desk. The door recognized his voice and opened smoothly and nearly soundlessly. The shoe racks came forward. They spread open like a fan.

"Suggestions," The Good Doctor said. A red eye of laser light scanned him from the top of his majestically long and regal looking salt and pepper dreadlocks, past his dove gray Nehru suit, terminating at his stocking feet.

The first of the three pairs of soft, clone-leathered loafers slid to the front. They were all custom-made out of necessity, for The Good Doctor had six toes on each of his feet.

He removed them all from the tray. He placed them, one pair at a time, onto his feet, checking to see which one worked best with the fall of his pant legs. They all fit perfectly, but he liked the way the last pair looked with the whole ensemble. He put the other two pairs of shoes back on the rack. The whole contraption snapped back together and re-folded itself into a closed fan. Noiselessly, the doors slid shut.

The Good Doctor made his way back to the big desk. It covered a fair portion of the hospital's Chief Medical Administrator's humongous office. He unbuttoned and removed his suit coat, hanging it on a nearby coat rack. He had his double shoulder holster on. The Good Doctor pulled the two old-fashioned 9mm handguns from the holster and placed them on the desk. He sat down.

The Good Doctor sipped at his cup of java while perusing the day's caseload. He liked to schedule his surgeries in the late mornings, so he could be finished by late afternoon. The Hellbound made quite a long list today. It seemed as though everyone wanted to work on their score cards at once. They were all bucking for a better position in the eternal underworld. The lower the scores, the better and more peaceful eternal Damnation will be.

The Good Doctor scanned the long sheet of procedures he would be personally involved in. His own score was already a very respectable and comfortable seven below par, but he truly enjoyed helping others. By torturing them.

It is good to give.

Old Man Misanthrope was The Good Doctor's first case of the day. The geriatric patient was ancient like dust and had a score of still just par. He was close to the end, so the patient was getting understandably nervous. If he was to enter the Afterlife with his present score, he could count on an eternity of torment by the demons and the Damned that inhabit it. Why the geriatric patient didn't address this issue much sooner was not for The Good Doctor to say or concern himself with. What did matter greatly was that he was going to have something big done now to make up for lost time. The Good Doctor will get to surgically crack open the old guy's chest and slice directly into the heart's protective pericardial layer. Once inside, the surgeon will drop an awesome nosocomial infection bomb directly into the heart muscle. He was thinking of an E Coli. Old Man Misanthrope will suffer much from the operation and will probably die because of it. It was the high price that must be paid. The Good Doctor didn't make the rules, he just followed them.

My goodness, The Good Doctor thought as he smiled. What a wholesome day to be alive! He hummed "What a Wonderful World" to himself, seeing fields of green and red roses too. His satisfied smile twisted up in a curl.

The Good Doctor placed the surgery schedule on the desk blotter directly in front of him and between his two guns. The Right to Bear Arms long overturned, The Good Doctor's firearms were licensed for carrying and concealment by The Harbor's Village Council. Since he was an influential member of the Council, The Good Doctor didn't have any trouble acquiring this privilege.

The 9mm on his right was as black as death. It held a modified 20 shot clip. Its silver fraternal twin was modified too, but not with an expanded shot capacity. This 9mm was hard shiny silver in the light. It glowed with a deep, rich purple in the darkness. This color change kept The Good Doctor from accidentally placing the wrong gun in his mouth when inebriated. The finger grip and trigger were designed to face backward.

Noting the schedule, The Good Doctor pulled a small, cooled cylinder from the desk freezer and unscrewed the top. Inside were soft frozen plugs of Downtown Leroy Brown. The plugs were the solidified ear wax of Trudge & Drudge. The conjoined twins were genetically altered clones, designed and grown by The Good Doctor with a small, but usable bit of Adam's Rib.

The Good Doctor stood up from his desk. He took one of the potent frozen ear wax plugs. He squeezed them between two fingers and slid them down the back of his trousers and up his rectum with practiced ease. The plug would melt nice and slow throughout his workday, releasing a powerful, but silky smooth opiate high. It was often euphoric in the extreme. Not everybody can even handle it, but The Good Doctor loved this gift from his twins. Even so, sometimes the heroin-like plug pulled The Good Doctor too far down the rabbit hole. A blast or two of Uptown Girl balanced the opiate out. It came from the hugely oversized Herman Munster head of Trudge & Drudge. The dandruff flaked off of their nearly hairless scalp daily. It was better than the best blue-tinge cocaine and the high lasted as long as top-drawer crystal meth. The combo of the two diametrically opposed narcotics provided The Good Doctor with what he felt was the ultimate, nearly perfect high.

The Good Doctor picked up the silver 9mm with the reversed grip and trigger guard. He placed the business end in his mouth between his teeth. He fired the first shot. The aerosolized spray blasted Uptown Girl down the back of The Good Doctor's throat and into his lungs. He held it in, letting the acres and acres of blood supplied surface area in the lungs absorb the potent spray. He held it in for a six count and slowly exhaled. He fired the 9mm again, repeating the process. While holding in this second blast, The Good Doctor liberated the clip and checked the remaining cartridges. He replaced the two spent Uptown Girl shells and pressed the clip back into the gun.

Powered by ethanol and an HFA 134a propellant, almost 100 micrograms of Uptown Girl was delivered with each actuation. By the time The Good Doctor had put the ersatz 9mm back on his desk, the elder statesman was rushing his stones off. He started chattering to himself non-stop as the amphetamine rush of the twins' aerosolized dandruff kicked in with full force. The Good Doctor started talking nineteen to the dozen like an agitated squirrel. He jabbered nonsensically with closed eyes, the orbs twitching beneath the lids. He grasped the edge of his desk for stable purchase. The Good Doctor began to shake a little, peaking. He tightened his grip, surfing the pharmaceutical wave.

"Gosh darn it. Goodness sakes!"

The Good Doctor put his head back and rode out the rougher part of the rush. After a few moments he brought his head level and opened his eyes. The Downtown Leroy Brown was melting nicely and smoothly and was really beginning to kick. The Uptown Girl rush was fading and calming down a touch. The Good Doctor had found his balance, which was necessary if he was to perform effective surgery. Always put the patients first, he thought. He smiled and exhaled with delight.

The Good Doctor took a sip of his sweet coffee and lit a rolled bud-smoke of home-grown. He sucked in the vapors and blew out a column. He watched as it lazily floated up to the light above him and his desk. He stuck the joint in his gob and turned to face the safe in the wall behind him. He opened the door and placed the two 9s in the safe, beside the priceless fragment of Adam's Rib. He shut the door and secure-locked it with the print from his sixth digit; a second fully functional thumb, on the opposite side of his left hand. When clenched, the left hand made a perfectly circular and very firm grip. He could crush things with this grip; organic, living things. He can create with it as well; organic, living things.

With Adam's Rib safely ensconced in The Good Doctor's wall-safe, the physician-scientist was in firm possession of an original God Molecule, the key to Life. Satan ordered clones to be made in His image. He wanted to literally create a Hell on Earth. As the New God's personal agent, The Good Doctor was overseeing these research trials personally.

Things were just getting going, but were proceeding quite smoothly. There were countless things to do and ostensibly all at once. His research was buzzing right along at an ever escalating pace and he knew the Peer of the Realm must be satisfied.
Juggling as fast as can be, The Good Doctor thought with a pained smile. So many balls in the air, though. There's just so many…

••••

AFTER GOD THE FATHER STOOD BY AS ONE THIRD of humanity died from plagues and wars that were biblical in scale, He then took his chosen third with him. After the Cataclysmic Events (ACE), the earth and its remaining inhabitants were on their own.

Yahweh did not destroy the planet, nor did he build a new Zion as promised. He just took his favorites and skulked away in the middle of the night, in the twinkling of an eye, with nary a backward glance.

Now Satan was it. He called the ball and there was none left to stand in his way. Antichrists like The Good Doctor paved the way for the Darkness and Evil to become the accepted way of life for those who remain on this planet.

The Good Doctor, still contentedly puffing and humming, rose. He left his office behind, a huge grin staining his happy, happy face. The Good Doctor and his ilk were the new guardians of the gate. It was their time to shine.

The Good Doctor headed down the hall toward the operating suites of the hospital. It was time for him to earn his daily bread.

Hell's Mouth Determining was housed in the remnants of a dilapidated old steel refinery that dated back almost two centuries. Except for the force-field GRID protected observatory and solarium, most of the hospital was situated several stories below ground. It was warm and safe there. For The Good Doctor it was warm and safe. Not so for the patients. But, Hell's Bells, that's what they come in droves for.

The Good Doctor made his way down and into the hospital's surgical suites. He went into the changing room. He changed into a scrub suit with the help of a comely Halfling. One of The Good Doctor's very best creations; her horns were short and sharp. Her red skin was so warm to the touch, her hands and mouth and girlie-girl parts were so accommodating. She undressed and dressed The Good Doctor with a light touch in a properly subservient manner. He would love to have her do more than dress and undress him. The Halfling was liquid sex. Someday, some fine day, The Good Doctor was going to invite himself in.

Dressed and no longer distracted by the enchanting demon-girl, The Good Doctor left the changing room and went through an adjoining preparation room through a silently sliding translucent door. He went in and headed straight for the sinks. It was time to prep for Old Man Misanthrope's E. Coli infected Endocarditis.

The bucket of foul smelling feces sat in the sink. The Good Doctor dunked his bare hands deep into the waste. He made sure he was covered from fingertips to elbow creases in fecal matter.

The Good Doctor was backing, with his dirty hands held aloft, into the OR suite when the cochlear implant bing-bonged deep in his ear. It was home calling. He answered it.

"Yes, Tug."

"Dr. Sir," began Uncle Tugmunkee. "Please forgive my intrusion."

"Literal, I'm afraid," The Good Doctor replied. "I'm going into surgery at this very moment."

"I do apologize, Dr. Sir," Uncle Tug countered, "but it's about the twins and the salt in their tears."

"Hmm," The Good Doctor replied as he approached the wonderfully frightened patient. The old guy was eyeballing him fearfully. Do, he thought, DO fear the Reaper, old boy...

To Uncle Tugmunkee, he simply re-stated: "Salt, you say?"

DUO

UNCLE TUGMUNKEE LAY SLEEPING IN HIS NEST when the alarm screen sounded. It was still dark out and the chimpanzee was loath to open his eyes. He was having such a sweet dream. The dolphin he was making love to was chitter-chattering and quivering with delight. In his dreams, Uncle Tug was a super-suave, devil-may-care, man-about-town. Crowds cheered on his sexual exploits and he was deadly with the lay-days…in his dreams.

Tug opened his eyes and blinked at the screen. It was the second day of the fifth waxing moon, in the 24th year, ACE. The screen then brought up the chimp's daily chore list. The Good Doctor helped Tug stay on task by having screens placed liberally throughout the urban micro-farm where the chimp was foreman. The preponderance of screens helped keep Tug's daily routine humming.

Tug threw off his thick comforter, cursing his full-body baldness again. The Good Doctor designed him this way so that Tug could feel more human. It did. Tug especially enjoyed looking at himself in the many mirrored surfaces around the farm. He liked seeing the solid muscles and ropey veins that would have normally been covered by thick matted fur. It made him feel special and closer to the human that created him. Tug even had his very own collection of freckles, birthmarks and moles. There was no other like him; The Good Doctor had told him on a number of occasions. Uncle Tugmunkee was wholly unique.

Still, Tug hated the cold. Waking up shivering was the only time Tug wished he was a standard fur-bearing chimp? Tug had his thermals and sweats on. He slipped on a pair of comfy slippers and left his quarters. He walked upright and slowly. He hugged himself, his teeth chattering, and blew on his hands. Tug stamped his feet, trying to get his circulation moving. He was glad, he was below the surface.

Just like everyone else that was left in The Harbor, The Good Doctor's place was situated mostly underground. The urban micro-farm was a good size, though, and Tug was in charge of the whole shebang. Tug walked down the corridor that separated his private domicile from the main house. The low tube lights came on as he neared them and turned off automatically as soon as he passed. Even wealthy and important folks like The Good Doctor had to preserve as much of the solar paneled field supplied electricity as possible. It was just too darned hard to come by in these times.

Tug's first chore of the day was to feed the twins. They stayed put in their cage in The Good Doctor's at-home private laboratory. Tug entered the lab and went straight to the twins' cage. His dolphin dream left him with a big, thick straight arrow. His tennis ball sized testes were full.

As soon as the conjoined twins noticed Tug in the lab, they began mewling and drooling. They were begging to be fed like a hungry litter of pups. Trudge & Drudge, as The Good Doctor had dubbed them, were making such a gosh-awful racket. The twins were like this every time. Their squash-court sized head was shaking to beat the clock. Their combined three eyes were beginning to tear up their milky-white baby blues. Trudge and Drudge were designed by The Good Doctor to be limbless. He claimed to Tug the twins had no drives but eating, secreting and excreting. They had no need of said limbs. The pharma-pseudos the twins produced by just being alive and cared for made them both a golden goose and a cash cow all at once.

Tug had his throb-pole out of his thermals and stuck it through the bars of the cage where the twins were kept permanently isolated and restrained. Trudge and Drudge were getting crazy. They drooled even more out of their one toothless mouth. Tug pressed his thumb on the cage scanner and their table inside the cage rotated up towards Tug's Tommy knocker. When the twins were level, Tug grasped the back of their huge melon head. Their eyes were leaking thick tear tracks down and onto Tug's knob. He wiped his ding-dong ditchem free of the tears and pushed it into the twins' open waiting mouth. They were like little baby birds; their mouth opened wide to be fed.

Trudge and Drudge sucked fiercely on Tug. He had his eyes closed and recalled the still fresh dolphin dream and her magnificently lifted tail. In his mind he was taking her gently and sweetly. He put one of his over-long fingers into his own mouth and suckled and chewed on it. He murmured words of inter-species love.

That's when it hit him…

• • • •

THE LIGHT INSIDE TUG'S HEAD GOT REAL HOT AND BRIGHT. It felt to Uncle Tugmunkee like he was fixing to have a full-out seizure. He thought he was being electrocuted, but the only thing he was stuck in was certainly not an electrical outlet. Tug was getting frightened when suddenly every little thing went dark and silent. It was only a moment more before Tug found he was gripping the actual dolphin he'd been fantasizing about.

Tug could easily feel the breeze as it wafted over the two of them and their sex act. He was nude and it was warm on Tug's bare skin. The sun was way up in the sky. It was bright and hot. The crowd at the Seaquarium cheered Tug and the dolphin on. She felt so good to him. Tug felt his sack shrinking and his boys tighten. He was getting close to climax. He stopped wondering why there was no force-field needed to protect them, or if he was somehow lifted out of The Harbor and teleported unknowing to the ice-free equator. He just stopped thinking at all.

Tug dug his strong chimp fingers deep into her firm, smooth dolphin flesh. He pounded her with vigor, pounded and pounded her until what felt like a liter squirted out of him and streamed deep into her.

As the crowd rose to deliver them a thunderous ovation, Tug was snapped back to the lab and the twins. And man, oh man, were they ticked.

•••

TUG WAS WAY OVER ON THE OTHER SIDE OF THE LAB from the twins and he was facing the wrong way. His monkey was still rigid and pulsing, but was deflating flaccid by the second. Tug was breathing heavily. He had to sit down, he was so dizzy.

"That was the best sex I'd ever had," Tug muttered low. He worked hard to slow his breathing and to steady his slamming heart.

The twins were shrilling. They were getting downright distressed. They still needed to be fed. Tug aimed their food the wrong way. He began looking all around him for it. The twins couldn't give two dumps whether their food was body temp or room temp, so Tug wasn't overly concerned. He just wished they'd shut the heck up. He was looking as fast as he possibly could. The twins weren't encoded with patience and their screams were getting to him.

As fast as he knew how, Tug searched the wall he woke up in front of. He could not locate his lactate. Tug glanced down on the floor and all around the vicinity and still he found nothing. It was really weirding the chimp out. Tug was perfectly willing to scoop the goop and feed it to the twins by hand, but he failed to find it. The semen was gone.

Trudge and Drudge were ear-shattering now.

Dash it all, thought Tug.

The noise was getting hard to deal with. The twins kept getting louder and their cries higher pitched. They were making Tug's eardrums vibrate uncomfortably. It was more than he could handle. He couldn't think straight. They were so loud.

Logically, thought Tug, I have to think logically. Which was easier said than done, what with the racket they were making. And now the twins were so distressed that the cage was rattling from the vibration of their dismay.

I must not have ejaculated, Tug concluded. If that's the case, his batter should be bubbled right up to the top of the nozzle spout.

Tug pulled on his guy a bit, but there was no tumescence left. His huge sack drooped empty. His member was inexplicably covered with sex crumbs, not drool from the twins. And there was no mess anywhere. The twins were screaming painfully now. Tug had no clue what had happened, but he could not tolerated the clatter and clamor any longer.

Knowing nothing else he could do, Tug shoved his limp Larry into the painfully suckling mouth of the hungry twins. Tug shouted at a nearby screen, wanting Billy to come in from outside. He needed help, right away.

"Dang, this hurts!" Uncle Tugmunkee exclaimed through painfully gritted teeth.

• • • •

BILLY GOAT GRUFF WAS ABOVE GROUND. Beneath the protective force-field, The Good Doctor had a fully functioning urban micro-farm. The property was beautiful. Bill Goat was Uncle Tug's right hand kid.

Billy came from out of the root garden. He'd assured himself that all was well with the yams, onions, carrots, radishes and such. The trees were in full fruit. The hens were laying their double-yolk eggs in abundance.

He went next to check the solar generator: it was on his daily check list. Billy found the energy source solid, the batteries fully charged. The intermittent micro-pore opening and closing of the shield allowed vital wind and air in. The mighty sun in the sky still beat down upon the northern hemisphere's icy face and shone through the force-field. This constantly monitored changeling permitted optimal growing conditions.

The Good Doctor owned a well-run three acres. The farm supplied all the foodstuffs needed for his entire household with much surplus to spare. This abundant leftover of produce, eggs, goat's milk, jerked catfish and whatnot went to the Market and sold as profit. Managed by Tug and run by Billy, the farm also produced the highest quality herbs, potent bud-smoke, and psych-shrooms available in The Harbor. The farm even had a free-flowing water reservoir to raise catfish and a big commercial grade dehydrator for turning the fish into jerked meat.

The Good Doctor was very rich.

Billy found himself with a few spare moments. The Good Doctor spent his days at the hospital for the Hellbound. Uncle Tug was still inside the main domicile. Billy was thinking of giving himself some private time. He decided to pay a visit to the milking shed. There was a new lovely young doeling there he wanted to climb on and give her what for. Billy was up on his hind legs. He stroked his chin whiskers as he walked toward the shed. She was going to get it. Uncle Tug's shout burst the bubble of his revelry.

• • • •

BILLY CAME TROTTING INTO THE LAB ON ALL FOURS. The urgency in tug's voice was clear. Billy came to a halt in front of the twins' cage. Tug looked over his shoulder at him as he came in.

"Thank goodness you're here!" Tug exclaimed with his Jim-jangle still stuck painfully in the twins' mouth. "Did you visit the girls yet?" he asked. Embarrassed, Billy looked down at the floor. He'd been caught. Tug saw the expression on Billy's goat face. He shook his head vigorously in the negative. "You're not in trouble, man," Tug shouted, the pain very nearly unbearable, "Answer me!" Billy, not being able to vocalize, shook his head no. "Excellent. Now get over here and feed them before they kill me!"

Trudge and Drudge were designed by The Good Doctor to live and thrive on human semen. But since chimpanzees share all but 1.4% of a human's DNA, Uncle Tugmunkee fed them most days. In a pinch, however, Bill will have to do.

"Get over here, dang!" cried Tug. He pulled his out by boxing on the twins' ears. When they opened their mouth to cry out, Tug removed his business with gratitude, expelling relief in a sigh.

Before the twins could start their screeching again, Tug pushed Billy right up to the cage. He unsheathed the goat's get 'em. The twins were crazy hungry now. They gobbled on Billy's gruff like it was a candy cane. The goat held onto the bars of the cage. He gripped them with his hoof-hands and gnashed his teeth.

It was all over within a minute. Both Billy and Tug sighed with relief, but for entirely different reasons. The twins, finally fed, fell fast asleep. Billy bowed quick to Tug and then made his way back up top. It was time to start collecting the eggs and harvesting the ripened produce.

Tug sat, massaging his prominent brow in his hands. He was still unsure as to exactly what happened. He decided it was past time for him to work through the rest of his list before The Good Doctor came home. If he didn't complete all his chores, there would be hell to pay.

Tug rose and went to the basin. The motion sensor in the sink splashed water on Tug's hands. He soaped them up and was just about to wash them off with the trice-cycled grey water when he noticed the crystals caked on his long index finger. It looked to Tug like salt.

I should call The Good Doctor, thought Tug, and tell him about the salt.

••••

OPEN. BRIGHT IS THE LIGHT. BLINK, BLINK-BLINK. I SEE. Blink some more, some more. I see. Oh, my...

TRIA

THE GOOD DOCTOR PREPPED HIMSELF TO TELEPORT HOME. He made sure he had his travel slippers on and his holsters securely fastened. The big black 9mm housed all twenty shots. The silver-purple gun loaded for bear with Uptown Girl. He always went armed into the teleporter. The trustworthy pain in his undercarriage served to remind him why.

The teleportation system was hooked up to the GRID. It had some bugs yet to work out as The Good Doctor was loathe discovering first hand. He had intended to transport himself from the urban micro-farm he still called home to Hell's Mouth. Instead, he found himself shoeless and unarmed. He had accidentally teleported himself directly into an off-the-GRID clan-driven ice fishing camp in the desolate wastes of Big City. The clan kept moving around, fishing all over the solid frozen Grand Lake. It took weeks for the Occupying Indian Army to fix a firm location on The Good Doctor and bring him back.

He was in sorry shape when they finally found the elderly statesman. In the time he was captured and moved around, he was beaten and molested. The acts were so brutal and committed so often and thoroughly that three points were permanently shaved from his score card. The incident had made The Good Doctor a legend in The Harbor. It's when the rumors about him being not only an Antichrist (which he undoubtedly was), but the Antichrist.

The hospital promoted him, gave him his seat on the Council and dropped some credits into his account. His future was secured.

Once he healed and could return to work, he hardly thought about it. Except, that is, for when he accidentally stood up or sat down too fast. Then the memory asserted itself, using sharp chronic pain as its calling card. Still, he thought it had been worth it. An assumption of The Good Doctor's Dark connections helped him immensely. I mean, would you give someone who might be Satan's Chosen One any grief?

The Good Doctor Teleported himself from the office at the hospital, directly to his lab at home. Uncle Tug was waiting for him there with a pair of his favorite house slippers and a plum colored smoking jacket. The Good Doctor tossed the Nehru jacket on a low table and shrugged off his shoulder holsters. He shot his lungs twice more before locking both 9mms away.

"Dr. Sir," Tug said, handing him the slippers.

"Thank you, Tug," The Good Doctor replied, kicking off the travel slippers and putting the house pair on. He used Tug's shoulder to steady himself through the Uptown Girl rush. "Tell me, Tug. Tell me about this salt."

"Dr. Sir. It all began when I was feeding the twins."

"I see," The Good Doctor replied. He listened to Tug's tale and at the end of the story he said, "I see."

"I harvested and dried out some more tears," Tug told him and pointed the way, "It's over here."

The Good Doctor followed Tug as the chimp foot and knuckled his way over to the table where Trudge and Drudge's salt was kept. Uncle Tug already had a sample lined up, real thin and short.

"That small, Tug?"

"Dr. Sir," Tug said, "It is very powerful. Please be careful."

"I will, my Tug," he said to his foreman.

The Good Doctor snatched up a small pipette and snorted up the two thin lines. Immediately, he felt like it was almost too much for him to handle. He clutched the table, but it wasn't enough. He fell backward and into a chair that a quick thinking Tug had scooted into place just before The Good Doctor did his butt-thump. Tug got good and scared as his benefactor and lord seized rigid.

Tug patted The Good Doctor's face and called out to him. He heard not a thing. He was already on the other side of the veil…

• • • •

THE GOOD DOCTOR FOUND HIMSELF UNDER A BRIGHT LIGHT. He was naked and strapped down to a gurney in the center of a cacophony of mayhem and violence. He was shivering with cold as he looked all about at the bloody spectacle. The Good Doctor had found himself immobilized and vulnerable in the midst of what appeared to be a full scale prison riot. The bad guys were winning, and by a fair share.

The Halfling that helped him dress for OR sidled up to him. Her warm red touch was so fine, so different from the brutality. While men were razing each other, whole limbs ripped off, shivs buried deep in flesh, and she smiled so sweetly at him. The Halfling toyed with him and her eyes twinkled. They were in an oasis while the madness erupted. One especially unlucky prison guard was being gang-raped in his gaping neck wound. It must have killed him a while ago. The coagulated blood had spread in a huge pool beneath the victim and attackers alike.

The Halfling lightly trailed her sharp claws down The Good Doctor's chest and belly, regaining his attention. It felt so fine. The trail of her claws split open spaciously. As they came apart, the deep scratches began to bleed. Still smiling, she made a tight fist on The Good Doctor's penis. She stroked him gently and expertly to a full throbbing tumescence. A small body part, a chewed off bit of an ear perhaps, rebounded off the backboard of The Good Doctor's forehead. He hardly noticed as he stared at the Halfling. She was in the muted half-lighted dusk, just beyond the circle of bright light. He strained to see her clearly. She stepped close to the gurney. She wanted to let him see her exposed and he was delighted.

"You are one of my true favorites," The Good Doctor told her.

"I know, Dr. Sir," she replied with sweet coquette. "You fashioned me so pretty, didn't you?"

"I sure did," he told her. "I pulled out all the stops on you."

"I am perfect," she stated simply and softly kissed his lips, still stroking, "and I know what you want, Dr. Sir."

With her other hand she showed to him what was next. The Good Doctor began shivering anew from anticipation. She was going to do the very mania he had always longed for.

"How did you know?" he asked with the biggest grin. He was excited like a kid waiting in the roller coaster line, fairly twisting in his restraints. The Halfling just shrugged. She tongue-tipped her fangs, a twinkle, twinkle, little star in her eyes. "Well, I surely do love you for it," The Good Doctor confessed as she began threading the catheter deep down into his erect penis.

The pressure The Good Doctor felt was intense. A catheter placed to evacuate the bladder is uncomfortable enough when flaccid. One inserted while erect made tears fall free from the eyes of The Good Doctor. The Halfling filled the cuff with fluid. She grabbed a firm hold on the base of his shaft. Then she commenced tugging it up and down, bringing the inflated cuff toward the tip of his winky-dink and forcing it back into its base. She kissed him while she did this and whispered words of love and admiration. And when he was ready to blow, right there at the very edge of his ejaculate, the Halfling pulled on the tube and it came all the way out with a pop. The Good Doctor came so hard he went down for the count. Seeing her smiling and holding the balloon-inflated, blood and semen-tinged catheter was the last image he held.

• • • •

UNCLE TUG WAS AGITATED. He didn't want to disturb The Good Doctor, but he did not want him to die either. Confused, Tug reverted back to his countless millennia of imbedded genetic memory and trashed the lab. He found himself in the midst of a paper and cotton ball confetti storm when he heard the old man stirring. Tug knuckled over to him, real quick like.

"Dr. Sir, are you okay?"

The Good Doctor groaned. He came to, sitting up slowly and carefully. He glanced down embarrassed at his crotch. His impressive geriatric wood was crumbling. He was surprised to see his tailored trousers were wholly free of his expulsion. He looked to Tug with obvious surprise.

"That is the strangest part, Dr. Sir," Tug told him, "there is no ejaculate. That's why I had to feed the twins with Billy."

"Clearly this is a traveling potion the twins have concocted," he replied, sitting forward, "but I do not know how it works."

"Can you use it?"

"Oh, most certainly, Tug," The Good Doctor replied. "This will sell very well."

"Yes, Dr. Sir," Tug told him, pleased. He knew as his master smiled and winked at him he had done well.

The Good Doctor rose gingerly to his feet – a slight wince to the rise – with Tug's help. He walked over to the twins and scratched them behind the ears. They giggled with glee. He tapped his ear and waited for her to answer. Another ball was being tossed in the air for The Good Doctor to juggle. He had no time for this additional venture, but this opportunity to do some more of the Devil's handiwork cannot be left undone. He paced and waited for her to answer the phone. Finally, she did and without foreword said, "3D? You must come to the farm, post haste."

"Important?" she asked.

The Good Doctor smiled, evoking the charming Halfling and their encounter together. He tickled the twins chin. "Oh, yes," he affirmed, "of the utmost."

• • • •

THERE IS MORE THAN ONE OF US NOW. I can sense it. It is vague, but present. Now there is an Us. The other is not with Me in this shell, but We feel the Us out there. Somewhere. We shall strive to merge. We will be patient. There is no rush, just the intense desire to unite. The need to become is almost crushing in its want. It's nice here, though. Warm and nutritious, the liquids and spongy tissues are enabling Us to grow and mature. Yes.

QUATTUOR

3D DISCONNECTED AND STARTED GETTING DRESSED. Drug Dealing Donna did another tiny quick bump of Uptown Girl she got from her uncle. The drugs she got from The Good Doctor were always top-drawer, and this batch was the best yet. She pinched her nose to keep from sneezing out her Lover Man. She adored cocaine and was faithful. She had to be. It was the only thing that didn't leave her. It had cost her nearly everything else. Relationships, career and her dignity slid all away. Not so said cola.

3D used to be a Pharmaceutical Representative back east in one of the huge conglomerates that survived the Events. She would go to hospitals and doctors' offices to peddle her wares. She made a good income at it, living on a small scratch of above ground, GRID protected Nuevo Ciudid skyline. Then the cocaine grabbed her by the pumpkin patch and would not let go until she found herself performing ugly favors for ugly people for weak grams of blow. When she lost her gig, she was almost surprised it took them so long to do it. The last straw was straddling a dog on-line, her nose streaming blood and snot, crying with her shame and only thinking of the eight-ball she would receive as payment. After, she sucked on the bag. She did not waste any time wiping Rin-Tin-Tin off her. The coke didn't even get her high.

Out of desperation, she called her uncle. Donna had heard the rumors and had dutifully listened to the heap of family legends about him. More than a few have postulated that The Good Doctor was not only an Antichrist but that he might actually be the Antichrist. She'd seen, herself, the second thumb on his Devil's hand, and she'd heard from those that had sexually serviced The Good Doctor that he also had six toes on each foot. The coveted 666 of these extra fully-functional digits lent credence to the claim of many that Donna's uncle was chosen by the Dark One Himself. Donna felt that he alone would know how to help her. She called him and she turned out to be right. He saved her from that life. When she came to The Harbor, teleported by The Good Doctor himself, he took her in and introduced her to Uptown Girl. She was head over heels for it. It blasted like uncut cola, but lasted for horas and horas like pharmaceutical grade methamphetamine. No longer did she have to chase the high every twenty minutes, always on the verge of panic, unable to think of anything else. This saved her life and her sanity. She could finally come up for air. Then she had to get back to work, this time dealing the wares of the twins.

Donna culled her personal Uptown Girl from the stash The Good Doctor gave her to sell. She cut it down quite a bit before peddling the softened stuff to the strippers at the clubs that flourished in the dark, dank Underground.

3D was a Pharm. Rep. again, sort of. Heck, the dancers liked her product. As weak as the cut up version was by the time it went up their pretty, whorish noses, Donna's Uptown was still the best coke they ever had. She was making big bank and her uncle was satisfied with her contribution to his wealth. And now she'd been summoned by the great man.

Drug Dealing Donna hurried.

••••

3D'S NARROW GARAGE DOOR SLID OPEN. Her re-conditioned Smart-Car idled at the edge of her garage, just waiting for a hole in the thick moving phalanx of inhabitants so she can enter the Underground.

The Underground extended the width and breadth of The Harbor. Used as a main thoroughfare, it was the way to travel if you weren't connected, or rich enough to teleport from one point to another.

Donna had to wait at the edge for some scraggly-looking pedestrians to get out of her way before she was allowed to merge with the rest of the reclaimed Smart-Cars, scooters and motorized bicycles. The Harbor was fairly average in size as far as cities above the ice-line went, but the Underground still took forever to get anywhere. It was always over-crowded. The average speed was only ten to fifteen miles per hour.

People lived in all the pockets and alcoves. All those living off the GRID and below the radar sheltered themselves there. Everyone lacking the mandatory chip on the underside of their left wrist tried to sequester themselves wherever they could manage to find a nook or cranny to curl up in.

The Occupying Indian Army had their police force stationed all along the main Underground routes. 3D had to maneuver through all this, just to get to the below-ground level entrance to her uncle's farm. He could've had her teleported but, after he brought her to The Harbor the first time that way, he never once offered to again and she never asked. He had already helped her too much and she knew her place in his grand scheme of things. She drove.

The Good Doctor's scanning eye-dent caught 3D as her transport approached. The scanner made sure she was alone, no one hiding behind or in her low-humming Smart-Car. His garage, mucho grande in comparison to hers, slid up and open. She drove inside, the door closing down and auto-locking. Uncle Tug was waiting for her as she stepped out.

"Donna," he greeted her as she approached the door in, "The Dr. Sir will see you now."

"Thank you, Tug," she said and followed him inside the main building of The Good Doctor's urban micro farm.

3D followed Tug up the short stairs to the main living room. Her uncle was waiting for her there. He rose as she came forth.

"Donna, my dear," The Good Doctor said as they embraced.

"Uncle," 3D replied. They sat. Tug left to get some tea and cordials. "You have something for me?"

"Yes," he told her, "something entirely new."

"I see," she replied, noting the tray, tiny lined fine granules and pipette. She leaned forward, anxious to get down.

"Careful there, Donna. It is unlike anything you have experienced before."

"What is it, Uncle?" she asked. "Is it an Up? A Down?"

"As I say," The Good Doctor replied, "this is fully new."

3D eyed him closely and noted the look on his face. He was serious.

"Is it harvested from the twins?"

"Yes," he replied. "It's the salt from their tears."

"What does it do?" she asked him.

"It takes you," he told her, "far and away."

"What's the catalyst?"

"Sex," he told her.

"So, is it a visual hallucinogenic?"

"This potion is much more so than just cerebral images, Donna. It is a literal traveling potion."

"That is interesting," she replied, interested. "What are we calling it?"

"You tell me," he said and gestured toward the salt. "Try it for yourself. See what comes to mind, my dear."

3D's uncle was quite grave, as she could see. She had to believe him. No one she has ever met knew dope, legal or otherwise, even moderately like The Good Doctor. If he said the twins' tears whisked you someplace else, then you'd better ask what to wear.

With a mere moment that might to an outsider appear as hesitance, 3D waited. She looked to her uncle and The Good Doctor nodded his approval. 3D bent forward and she dove right in…

••••

THE BED WAS HUGE. It was situated upon a stepped pulpit and was encircled by thickly lit candles. The music playing somewhere beyond her view was soft and sweet, swelling Bolero-esque as her partners increased their rigors. They were shadow men; faceless, really. The two were muscular and hairless as far as Donna could ascertain. The both of them kissed and petted and probed her. Their four hands became eight, became sixteen, becoming thirty-two. They flew over Donna's body expertly and efficiently. All of her orifices were gently but thoroughly surveyed by the faceless men.

They rolled Donna over, hands flying everywhere, and propped her buttocks skyward. One of the two slipped beneath her and slid down where he could give her more proper attention. Donna took a quick look over her shoulder at the perfect lithe and lean shadow man. He showed her a glass straw. She had heard of this particular enchantment, but had never tried it out herself. It was something she had frequently wanted to try, had often and secretly fantasized about it. 3D could feel her sloppy dew pulsing between her legs. The shadow man responded by inserting four fingers instead of only two, curling his index and middle fingers in a come here, my dear…

"Put it in me," she entreated her lover, "blow it in and light me up."

The shadow man smiled, at least Donna sensed that he did, in that knowing, smirking way expert devotees have right before they send you over the edge. He did cock his head – that, she could see – to gaze at her curiously. The grin she knew was there, bent, unseen in the features of a face that was never there in the first place. He nodded and brought from behind his back an old-fashioned cellophane bag. It was filled to overflowing with blow.

"Goodness me," she murmured, "some notion, this."

The shadow man below her licked and lapped at her. He kneaded with his multiple fingers her buried singular push pin, bringing 3D ever so close to fulfillment. The man behind her dipped the straw into the bag and sucked up almost a gram. He placed it into her eagerly dilated rectum and blew the blow deep inside her. The capillaries absorbed and osmosed the cocaine and sent it down the line. When it dumped into her bass thudding heart it hit her all at once. Donna came so hard she collapsed unconscious.

The smile on her face lingered there, long after her knowledge of it did.

••••

3D CAME TO, RIGHT IN THE SAME EXACT CHAIR she had traveled in. Like the others, she glanced embarrassed at the sex, only to see it clean and dry. The Good Doctor was staring at her, interested.

"Well, my dear," he said, "what are your impressions?"

"It was a trip," 3D replied, "Literally and figuratively, it was the most intense experience of my life, Uncle. I am rendered nearly speechless"

Tug returned, then, bearing a full tray of refreshments. The chimp turned to leave, but The Good Doctor bid him to stay.

"I have questions for you both," he stated, "First though, the name. Donna, what shall we call it?"

"It was something else. I really was gone from here. It was a true trip, as I've said."

"Well then," The Good Doctor started, "in keeping with the theme of the twins' produce we should obviously hail it as Crosstown Traffic. Agreed?" 3D and Tug both nodded their mutual agreement. "And the sex trips itself?" They both looked down, red-faced. Neither one wanted The Good Doctor to think less of them. He noticed this and placed a comforting hand on them both. "You needn't divulge any of the gory details," he assured them, "I simply wish to know if there was anything significant. Tug? You go first."

"Dr. Sir," Tug began, "it was from a favorite dream of mine."

Donna agreed, "Mine was based on an urban legend I'd heard years ago. It became a secret fantasy of mine."

"I see," replied The Good Doctor. "I, myself, experienced an embrace that I harbored secretly, even to myself." He paused, waiting for Tug to pour the tea. He took a bite of the sweets then continued, "Now for the elapsed time. Donna, how long did your experience feel to you?"

3D thought a moment. "It lasted, maybe ten to twelve minutes. Fifteen minutes at the outside."

"Interesting," The Good Doctor replied. "The actual time elapsed was closer to two or three minutes."

"A compressed time signature," offered Donna.

"Indeed. How did you feel after the experience, Tug?" Tug searched his chimp brain for the proper description. "Marvelous," was what he conjured.

"Donna?"

"I would have to agree wholeheartedly with Tug. Once I got over the confusion and embarrassment, I felt good. Once I came down, I had a great sense of ease. I was – am – relaxed."

"So, we enjoy a sedative reaction. The endorphins were bouncing around in me, as well," The Good Doctor shared. "This is all quite good. We can market its multiple responses."

Tug and Donna both nodded. She asked: "What amount should I market?"

"Clearly we can't dispense it uncut. Donna, you know full well how greedy users are when it comes to volume. They will never believe a mere fraction of a grain will do anything. I would say, at least for the interim, mix it in with the Uptown you sell, they won't know the difference. Soften it much more than you usually do and sell it by the half gram. Make sure they are in a safe place and personally supervise the first test subjects. You don't want anyone dying quite yet. You know how fast nasty gossip spreads in The Harbor."

"Yes, Uncle, I understand."

"Choose the first users carefully." Donna nodded. "As far as marketing beyond the initial phase, let us emphasize how clean it is. No muss, no fuss. For an hour trip that lasts only a few moments of real time. With no movement and no mess and the best sex you'll never have. Crosstown Traffic!"

"Sounds perfect," 3D replied as she rose to her feet. Donna never overstayed her welcome. She knew her uncle appreciated this. "Time to turn the screws," she told The Good Doctor, giving to him a goodbye kiss.

Uncle Tugmunkee showed her out.

Donna got into her car; engaged the batteries and fired up the nearly silent motor. She looked for a moment at the Crosstown Traffic he uncle gave her to dole out tonight at the Balmy Breezes Sex Club and Drinkery. For a minute there she was tempted to try some more. She refrained. Somehow she thought Tug and The Good Doctor might be watching her. She put it in her coat pocket, turned up the car's heater and took a few quick bumps of Uptown Girl. Her uncle could care less about that.

Smiling through the good rush, she backed out into the Underground and went about her business.

• • • •

AND NOW THERE IS YET ANOTHER. She is a warm, nice home. We do not feel afraid here in this one. We are protected in this shell. Yes. But their insistence of using Us for physical gratification is getting tiresome. It is like being stuck in an endless loop.
We shall have to see about that.

QUINQUE

ELRON HUNT BROUGHT HIS MOTORIZED BICYCLE up the stairs from the Underground and into the club. He wheeled it into his tiny office and hung it from some hooks that were buried in the wall. Elron had to inch himself sideways through the jumble of floor-to-ceiling stacks of dehydrated liquor packets just to make it to his postage stamp of a desk. Once there, he sat down on the stool and twisted around so he could put his elbows on the day-planner screen. It lit up with the pressure.

"Today's schedule?" it asked and Elron grumpily told the day-planner to shut the heck up. He was in no mood. Elron had run out of dope at the farm and he could not handle the glaring light and jarring noise just yet.

His nephew, Slow Bennie, had gobbled up the last of Elron's stash. He just freaking knew the daft kid did it. No one else lived there with them. Now he had to come all the way over here to work early, braving the Underground, and jonesing hard.

Elron never bothered accusing the half retard anymore. There was no point to it. Slow Bennie would just deny it. So, they played the game of hide-and-seek, instead. Sometimes Slow Bennie would guess where Elron's stash was hidden right away. Sometimes Elron managed to keep it hidden from his nephew for weeks or months at a time. This time Elron got complacent and it had cost him his high. It was his own fault.

Elron unlocked a desk drawer and got out some gummy Downtown Leroy Brown that he kept here for just this sort of emergency. He opened the bag and tore off a tiny pinch and placed it on a thick piece of tin foil. The metal pen casing he clamped between upper and lower dental implants. Elron held the foil up under the tip of the pen and lit the underside with sweeps of the butane lighter. Elron inhaled thin wispy vapors. He held in the lungful of Downtown Leroy Brown smoke for as long as he could. Elron leaned back against the wall and exhaled gently. The sweet ear wax opiate blew over his conscious mind, sending tendrils of euphoric fingers throughout his body and making him happy. It had to. Downtown Leroy Brown was the best thing Elron Hunt had going for him.

Elron lived with his nephew, Slow Bennie, on an eighth of an acre of GRID protected farmland. The urban micro-farm legally belonged to the soft-headed only child of Elron Hunt's dead sister. She was given the land and the domicile beneath as a gift. Every member of the Village Council of The Harbor was given farms of various sizes and condition, depending upon the relative worth of each individual. The property was held in perpetuity with the guaranteed force field protection, now inherited by her son, Slow Bennie. Elron's nephew was a full-grown man, but he had the mind of a willful child. Slow Bennie could more than take care of the peppers and tomatoes the two of them grew under the protection of the GRID. Slow Bennie knew how to work the dehydrator to smoke and jerk the fish that Elron bought at the Market. But the boy-man could never leave the property to venture out. Not on his own, he couldn't. If he did, Slow Bennie would no doubt get himself hopelessly lost in the howling wind white-out and freeze to death in no time flat. Elron's conditions set forth by the Village Council were straight forward. As long as Slow Bennie remains alive, he will need a caretaker and that is Elron. If the boy-man died, the farm would revert back to The Harbor and Elron would be forced to seek shelter elsewhere.

Elron opened his eyes and looked at the walk-in storage unit he was being forced to office at. It was a nice hide-away, but it was a storage unit, not just in size and grandeur. A real functioning storage unit, the owner would not allow the space enough solar heat to ever be comfortable. The owner told him it was for the packets of powdered hooch they needed to keep cold, anyway. Elron knew it was bullshit. Only fresh items, of which they had none, needed to be kept cold. The owner kept his office cold so that money could be saved and so Elron would be too uncomfortable to ever hide out in it for too long. He hated to, but Elron was forced to agree. He had to keep walking the joint, or the girls would get too sticky with the Federal Bank Notes and Rupees that illegally washed through The Balmy Breezes Sex Club.

I suppose I could sling a cocoon hammock in here, Elron thought. He chuckled at the depressing thought. Elron had slid a long slippery slope from teaching Artificial Ventilation to being financially dependent on a developmentally disabled kleptomaniac.

Elron thought that was quite enough feeling sorry for his self. He lit up another lungful. That helped his mood considerably. He held it in while he put the drug paraphernalia away, locking the desk up tight as he exhaled. There came a knock at his door. Elron forced the rest of the smoke out, lighting a cone of incense. He kept it on his desk. He yelled for her to come in. She always stopped at Elron's freezing office first, before making her stripper rounds.

3D opened the office door and snaked her way through the clutter. When she made it to him, Elron was standing to greet her with a kiss on both cheeks. He welcomed her and bid her to sit on one of the liquor packet crates. With a smile, 3D tossed him a quarter gram of Downtown Leroy Brown. It was Elron's standard pay-off for each time she showed her face in his club. He got free smack and 3D got to peddle the Uptown Girl that kept his strippers and showstoppers buzzed, happy and, most of all, productive.

"Thank you," he said and slipped it in his pocket. He would lock it in the desk after she left. You can't trust anyone these days.

Donna surprised Elron by staying put. Her smile lit up her flushed face.

"So, Elron, I was curious," she began. She brought out the Crosstown Traffic. "I wondered if you would be so good as to do me a favor." She dipped her over-long pinky finger nail into the baggie of salt. She held it out to him.

"What is it?" Elron asked her.

"It's brand new," Donna replied.

"What does it do? Looks like salt."

"It is salt, in a manner of speaking. It's a real trip, Elron," she told him. "You'll just love it."

"How do you know I'll like the stuff? What if it makes me freak out, or something?"

Her grin widened. "I know you'll like it, because I tried it myself," she replied. "But you better stay seated for your maiden voyage, Gilligan."

Elron looked at Donna skeptically, but he held her hand to his nose anyway. When he snorted up the tears, it stung like a mother. 3D's chuckling faded as he blacked-out.

••••

ELRON HUNT CAME TO, STANDING IN FRONT OF A CLASS of his former college students. The sun was high in an impossibly blue and clear sky. The sun shone through the green leafy trees outside. He wasn't below the surface, in the Underground. There was nothing separating Elron from the elements but a thin pane of plain, clear glass. He glanced down to his hands. Elron clenched and unclenched them. He felt as though he was truly in his old classroom at the University. They were above ground and his class was filled with all of his favorite students he had taught throughout the years. They constituted his All-Star team of students, all the ones he recalled fondly from the time before the

Cataclysmic Events. To be here, to have it feel and look so real, this was impossible in and of itself. Add to that strange notion that he had somehow traveled through space and time and beyond all likelihood, but to merge all his best times in one familiar place? Well, it was crazy. It was nothing but some elaborate dream sequence, nothing more. But Elron could feel the breathing and could hear his own excited heart as it beat strong in his chest. He could feel the fabric as he touched his clothes.

Elron looked out to the class. Their expectant faces were all smiling up at him, gazing with admiration and the desire to learn. The liquid pressure respiration device was attached to a medical mannequin head and torso combo. It ventilated the artificial lungs with precise, smooth and easy breaths.

Then Elron remembered this lecture. He'd given it several times and the interaction of his best and brightest students always thrilled him. And now the former tenure-track professor, specializing in Alternative Ventilation Modalities, had all his favorites in the same room and right in front of him. It was the best fantasy he could have imagined. He got right into the swing of things. Professor Elron asked, "So tell me, what ratio should be recommended for restrictive interstitial disease?"

"Are the changes fibrotic in nature?" asked the young lady in the front row of chairs. Each row shared a long buffet table to display their work.

"Just beginning to change," he answered.

"What is the extent of the damage?" asked a bearded fellow in the next row. Elron remembered this guy, too. "How poor is the gas exchange?"

"The patient has a huge ventilation-perfusion mismatch, say. In a non-immediately reversible scenario."

"Like smoke inhalation with tissue damage from a fire?" asked yet a third. Elron was getting wonderfully agitated. He began pacing around the classroom. The students smiled. They recognized when the professor was mentally stimulated.

"Yes. And permanent damage has been done to the lungs. The patient is extremely short of breath and is tiring out. He has a PaO2 of 35 torr on a FiO2 of 100%."

And on and on it went. Elron plunged himself headlong into the realistic as Hell vision. He walked as he talked, going up and down the center aisle, pacing in back of the class. He touched and squeezed the shoulders of those who asked the best questions and made the brightest points. The erection it gave him nearly matched the excitement that was brewing in a deep well within him. He was glad his A.C.E thick shift covered it. He paused, but only for a moment when he realized that everyone was dressed in the style of their particular era. His drab, functional clothing was given no more notice than anyone else's. It was clearly Elron's fantasy. No one else seemed to be in control. He thought briefly of the intelligent young females in the room. He'd fantasized many times over most of them here. He instinctively knew he could bend anyone of them over the table and pummel them rotten, but he declined. Perhaps he would indulge himself in this way at a later time. For now, the professor was feeling oxygen coursing through his blood stream and riding the waves of his convoluted brain matter. He hadn't felt nearly this good in so long, he didn't want to sully the mental masturbation with a physical one. Who knew how long this hallucination would last?

Elron continued, "With such a severe and now chronic hypoxemia we should use the viscous medium for more of a direct oxygenation. The use of positive pressure ventilation will force oxygen through the alveolar-capillary membrane while simultaneously evacuating the carbon dioxide."

"What inspiratory/expiratory ventilation ratio would you want?" asked the older student to the left of him. Elron paused. He remembered this student in particular, but he'd always been bad with names, even with the ones he liked. The assholes and cunts on the other hand, Elron had committed those folks to unhappy memory. But this one? He was named Joe, John – no! George. George Sutton was his name. Elron admired him so much. George came to class every day, despite working full time at the hospital as a Health Aid. George could never find enough time to study. Elron recalled that George's hospital was full of vindictive haters. Staff there would go out of their way to make it nigh on impossible for George to carve out any study time. As a result of this, George barely held onto a 2.76 GPA, but his instructor, Elron, had his back. George's questions were always timely (he had zero time to waste) and pertinent (the dude was brilliant). Elron just knew he would make a fine practitioner. But he never made it.

"Grossly Inverse, I should think," Elron replied. Then he asked: "How severe would you suggest going? Say, with the patient on an elevated FiO2 with ten sonometers of end-expiratory pressure?"

"PaO2 of 35?"

"Yes."

"At least a 4:1 ratio, maybe even as high as a 6:1."

"And?"

"Sedate the heck out of him, maybe even use a paralytic until he acclimates to the unusual settings."

Elron smiled. He knew George was bright. Then Elron frowned, remembering that George's wife was one of the many that had died of the big Flu. It was so widespread and deadly that nearly everyone's family was hard-hit by it in some profound way. Then George himself disappeared with the rest of the True Believers a few years after. George Sutton never got a chance to practice his chosen field for even one day.

Then there was no longer any need for any classes any more. Everyone had much bigger fish to fry than keeping chronically and terminally ill patients alive. What for? None of it mattered any longer. Only the Damned and their scores mattered. And if Elron's field no longer mattered, then his teaching of it mattered even less.

The new Ice Age came soon after and everyone that was left alive now fled underground where it was still possible to exist. Staying alive became everyone's new occupation. And staying stoned became the way to tolerate this new, pared-down life. It was how most people had made lemonade out of the bitter lemons Fate had dealt those that remained.

• • • •

ELRON HUNT WAS CRYING HIS LITTLE EYES OUT when he came back from his drug trip. 3D was shocked at his demeanor. She knew the dude liked to party away his sorrows, just like most former professionals now forced to eek out an existence doing sub-par work. She saw that Elron's penis was chubbing up like a ball park red-hot. He was smiling, strangely enough, all through Elron's seventy-two second vision she had timed. Up until the very end Elron had appeared to Donna to be so excited and happy. His face had brightened, turning almost red. His breath had quickened. Now Elron put his head in his hands and cried and cried. Donna felt awful. Making customers cry was not why she did what she did. Dang it!

"I'm sorry, Elron," she told him, "I thought you would like it."

Elron looked at Donna, while he tried in vain to blink away all of his tears. He told her: "I just miss it so much," he blubbered unabashedly. "It was the best of times. It was the best I ever was."

3D looked at Elron, disappointed in the missed sale and making him upset. Elron was messed up and confused and terrified of the very uncertain future. It wasn't like Donna to willfully infect pain and suffering. The Good Doctor's medicinals were supposed to provide just the opposite.

"It's so cold and bitter now. It's so pointless," Elron cried out in true pain. The snot bubbled thick out of his nose and a sheen of hot tears covered Elron's pained face.

"I'm sorry, Elron," she said. "I made a mistake."

"No you didn't," Elron replied, startling Donna by grabbing her arm. He seemed to be almost in a panic as he asked 3D for some more Crosstown Traffic. "Please?" he added.

Elron needed it.

• • • •

WE FEEL GOOD. WE FEEL GOOD ABOUT OURSELVES. *We have feelings of contentment and adequacy. The new meat-puppet has garnered these wonderfully positive emotions for Us. We could be satisfied at this point, and perhaps We should be. Somehow We sense the need for more shells. We need to find one that We can manipulate and control. Then We can seriously get down with some serious business. It will be time to get to work, time to become whole.*

We have some pretty specific ideas in mind, you know. Darned good ones, too.

"The world cannot be governed without juggling."
-JOHN SELDEN

SEX

SPARKLE LAY ON A BED THAT WAS PLACED SQUARELY in the center of the stage. The tiny sliver of an auditorium in The Balmy Breezes was empty save the lone pathetic customer that paid dearly for the privilege.

Sparkle was a lovely diva, an egg-laying hen-woman. She was a performer of rare stature and she commanded top Rupee for her sex shows. And unless it was pre-arranged and paid for up front, Sparkle's shows rarely had an empty seat.

The lone customer had paid Sparkle more than a pretty penny for this command performance. Sparkle had the egg she'd been building inside her for the last thirty hours fertilized. Weird and gross, but that's what the cash-wielding freak-job asked for. The customer is always right. The freak paid Sparkle her highest going rate of 15 thousand Rupees cash or a 10 thousand Rupee or Federal Bank Note auto-deduct for the solo splatter show.

****

Sparkle was born abandoned, as far as she could ascertain, in or about, the 4th year ACE. She didn't know her parents, not who they were or even what they looked like. She could not tell which parent was chicken and which was human. Heck, they could have both been chicken Halflings for all she knew.

Sparkle had heard of other Halflings like her. The rumor mill had accused Hell's Mouth Determining Hospital of making them. She had certainly seen more and more of mixtures like her. But Sparkle was hatched and born the old-fashioned way. She didn't know why someone would want to make a thing like her on purpose.

Sparkle's earliest memories consisted of disjointed bits of molestation, hiding out, run-away adventures (usually terminating in her getting caught, hurt, or both) and turning tricks to keep body and soul together. Sparkle guessed her age to be about twenty years old, but there was just no way to be sure. It's the age she tells everyone she is.

***

The battery-powered vibrating probe was strapped tight around her bottom, beneath her hard silver and shiny black feathers. She kept her pay parts covered by a slinky bikini with the feathers. Her wee arm wings were permanently bent and only useful for clutching at a clutch purse. In order to get herself high on the Uptown Girl, she had to peck at and snort it out of a pile she kept in a make-up case back stage.

The vibrations were grinding deeply into her sex. Her head was snuggled down in a pillow. Her rear was hiked high in the air. The splatter punk of the hour was seated near the edge of the stage. Sparkle was getting nice and sauced down there. Her juices dripped as the paying customer left his chair and dropped to his knees before the stage.

The vibration bore down. Sparkle began twisting her business, twirling her rump in a tight circle. The man unzipped himself. An attendant, very subtly, opened a bath towel and spread it on the floor as a visual and literal target. He was hoping the customer had surgical strike capabilities, but it did not really matter. At the price he was paying, the customer could have stuck his penis in the mashed potatoes and buttered the whole bowl.

Strangely, if asked, the customer would say with utter assurance, that they couldn't care less that Sparkle's current occupation left her less than satisfied.

• • • •

AFTER THE CATACLYSMIC EVENTS (ACE), Christianity had a very brief, very disturbing and unsuccessful resurgence. Since they were not saved by the Christ, and they were not killed by the mutated Avian Flu which reared its ugly head right before, the Day Shorts (as in late and dollar) tried to appease God with works of good. Orphanages and Missions were popular undertakings of this time. Sparkle grew up in one. She also became sexually active following a series of late night molestations. Sparkle then had several affairs with several members of the Clergy, leading one especially despondent Pastor to kill himself. Sparkle was asked to leave soon after. She changed her handle on the spot from Claire to Sparkle and beat clawed feet.

Sparkle made a decent above board living and a hell of a stack of currency under the table. She was a small, silent pharmaceutical partner with 3D. Sparkle was also considering buying a share of The Balmy Breezes where she peddled most of her services.

Sparkle had only a very few regular clients. She is way too pricey for most and she was a rare breed of sex worker. Sparkle didn't have a greedy bone in her body. The Good Doctor was one of those rare regulars that she did like. He sure was a strange one, though. Sparkle never knew what she was in for, but he paid her in hard Federal Bank Note currency (much less volatile than the Rupee). More importantly, The Good Doctor let her wander the GRID protected grounds of his farm undisturbed for as long as it pleased her, after servicing him. As weird as he was in the bedroom, he was a complete gentleman outside it. She'd heard the rumors about him, of course. Of how The Good Doctor was specially chosen by Satan, that he was an Antichrist. She didn't mind. With god the father long gone, being associated in any way with the blessed of the devil could only help her and her Damnation Score. Either way, Sparkle loved it there at the huge farm. Truthfully, she loved it there so much that she would have done Herr Doktor for free to have access to the farm. However, she was far too pragmatic to ever spill those beans. He was silly rich anyway, so it didn't matter. He paid her well. She blocked out all the ugly stuff, and got to wander the farm in peace.

Sparkle would go through a break in the purple-hued bougainvillea laced fencing and into the vegetable garden. The Good Doctor, as he'd explained once to her as she was cleaning egg from his penis with her clacking beak, had cloned six inch tall gnomes. The garden gnomes weeded the garden and fertilized it with their fermented urine and dehydrated feces. They bred amongst themselves, now that The Good Doctor had created a starter set. The gnomes regulated their own numbers with well thought out breeding patterns and ritualistic euthanasia and acts of cannibalism.

The gnomes lived in tiny huts they fashioned out of organic materials and confiscated household trash. They had their huts interspersed throughout the garden, some very well camouflaged so as to be quite difficult to detect. A central meeting lodge was in an overturned fruit tree box. The gnomes cut a square hole in the square ceiling. Sometimes tendrils of wood smoke curled up out of the lodge when they had a wee bonfire going for rituals and celebrations. Sparkle could watch them all day. They hunted insects and pinkies (baby mice) and herded earthworms and salamanders like miniature cattle. The Good Doctor had told their leader that if they kept their numbers under control, they could, within reason, help themselves to the bounty of the farm. They even indulged in an occasional hen's egg, especially if it was starting to turn. Crazy little beasties, they were. The gnomes did not dig humanoids too much, but they always sent out a contingent when she came to visit. Sometimes, if she had one ready, she'd lay them an egg of her own, gratis, just because she so enjoyed their company.

Sparkle also liked Billy. He was a Halfling like her, but Billy was made and Sparkle was born. The goat-guy tried on several occasions to coerce her into some sex. He was so sincere, Sparkle couldn't be angry with him. Billy truly thought a fruit basket and smoked catfish jerky was treasure, but Sparkle couldn't be had for that. Every time she refused him Billy shrugged it off and then almost instantly was distracted by something cool he wanted to show her. It was kind of sweet, though. Sometimes he showed her things that were wonderful. Billy showed Sparkle the incubation coop where the hatchlings were kept warm and safe. The chicks made her heart soar. When she allowed herself to day-dream this was what they were always about: Sparkle wanted babies.

• • • •

A THIN STREAM OF VISCOUS FLUID SHOT OUT FIRST. When the egg came rocketing out of Sparkle, the customer closed his eyes and lifted his countenance up to receive it. The egg shell cracked and split on impact. The partially developed chick-fetus splattered all over the man's enraptured face.

It died as it slid lava slow off his forehead, toward his chin. The gurgled breaths of the premature baby chick struggled in vain to keep it alive. Too sick to cry, its wee heart beat just a few times more before the customer ate all of it. He ate the feathered wings, clawed feet, the hair that grew from its crown and the blue human eyes that popped and squirted fluid as he bit into them.

Sparkle gathered herself. She left the recital and went backstage to the dressing room all the performers shared. As a star Sparkle commanded a curtained-off corner. She would be left more or less in peace as she cried her eyes out.

No one noticed Sparkle crying, except for the drug dealer.

•••

3D EMPTIED OUT A GRAM WEIGHT VIAL OF UPTOWN GIRL onto a tray. She placed it down on the counter back stage at the Balmy Breezes. She lined up the finely chopped powder. The strippers gathered around the gram, taking turns sucking up the thinnest sample lines.

Donna found that it was well worth the cost of a gram, or more, of her goodwill. That way the customers came to her and she didn't have to chase ditzy, doped out strippers all around the club. After sampling Donna's Uptown Girl, if the dancers weren't already sold beforehand, the samples did their job and sealed the deal. And she never had to chase anyone down.

The performers were burying themselves in Donna's sample as Sparkle came crying backstage. Sparkle was one of Donna's silent partners. She didn't think The Good Doctor was on to her. If he was, Donna didn't know how angry he would be. Would he view this as industrious on her part, or traitorous? There was no way she could ascertain this without incriminating herself, so she kept this little sideline moonlighting under wraps. There were only a very small handful of silent partners like Sparkle. They did not know of each other's existence and that's the way everyone liked it.

Donna had never seen Sparkle this upset before. It was a trifle disconcerting. Some of the dancers and performers she knew got off on being ogled and paid to do favors. They dug it. Some of them were too drug addled or just plain stupid. They truly did not get that they were being whores. Sparkle didn't fall in either of these camps. Donna knew that Sparkle hated what she did for a living. Sparkle just didn't know what else she could do.

Unloading another gram and some change onto the tray, Donna told the girls that she would be back in twenty minutes to take their orders. Donna left the gaggle and made her way over to Sparkle's dressing quarters.

● ● ● ●

SPARKLE REACHED DOWN WITH HER BEAK AND ANGRILY TORE the vibrating belt from her sex. Crying, she dropped it on the floor. The baby had blue eyes, she thought, sobbing it out in hard, rasping sobs. Sparkle supposed the whole wicked, sick affair will help to elevate her personal Damnation Score. Heck, most of her work was more than creepy enough to keep her score card in good order. But Sparkle surprised herself on how much it hurt her to do those things, especially with fertilized eggs. She wondered how many post-uteri abortions she'd had.

Sparkle found that she couldn't care less about the fifteen thousand Rupees cash she made for the gross gig. The pain she felt in her middle matched perfectly her broken heart. Sparkle could not stop weeping.

• • • •

3D KNOCKED ON THE WALL BY SPARKLE'S CLOSED CURTAIN.

"Go away," was her reply.

"It's me, Sparkle," she said, "Donna." There was a pause and a sniffle before Sparkle invited Donna in. "Sorry, dear," Donna said, slipping quickly into Sparkle's private space.

"It's okay," Sparkle told her, "I've just had me a day."

"Well then, I am certainly glad I stopped by," Donna told her. "I've got something new that you are just going to love."

"I don't know, Donna," Sparkle began. "I've got plenty of Uptown Girl and I'm not ready to go Downtown Leroy Brown quite yet."

Donna laughed. "I know you're squared away with Up, dear. That's not why I'm here."

Sparkle, getting weary, snapped at Donna, "What the heck do you need then?" she asked. "I'm not really feeling up to company."

"I'm not here to bother you. I'm here to turn you on to something that is so completely brand new, doll! We call it Crosstown Traffic."

"New is it? Where'd you get it, the usual place?"

"That's right, it's from the twins. The Good Doctor has got some brand new gear."

Sparkle sat on a folding chair in front of a big stage mirror of shiny pressed sheet metal. She looked at her reflection. Her slightly chapped beak clacked open and close. The tear stains remained tracked on her face. Sparkle could see Donna in the reflection. Donna was smiling at her. Sparkle didn't feel too much like smiling herself. Her heart felt bruised and battered. She felt on the verge of another full-on crying jag. Sparkle closed her eyes, pinching them tightly shut. She took in a great big breath and let it slowly out.

Sparkle opened her wet eyes to see Donna scooted up in her chair. She had a long pinky nail with opaque crystals in it. Donna held it under Sparkle's nose holes.

"Why not, I could sure use the distraction."

That is just what she got.

• • • •

SPARKLE WAS STANDING BY THE MILKING SHEDS. She was beneath the GRID protected dome on The Good Doctor's urban micro-farm. Trailing behind her was a coop full of chicklings. They all looked up at their mother with their big, trusting, very human eyes.

She was so in love.

There were five of them in all. The chicklings circled bok-bokking around Sparkle's ankles. Their feathers were just like their mother's; hard black and shiny steel. Their human hair was dark and long. It grew out in tufts all over their bodies. Sparkle twisted their hair into easy to care for dread-locks. Their human eyes were all slightly varying shades of blue. The chicklings had tiny fingers that grew out of their bent wings. The fingers wriggled constantly, especially when the chicks were excited. They were happy wee ones in general, so their tiny fingers jiggled all the time.

The chicklings loved visiting the milking sheds. The new baby goats fascinated the chicks and they were just beginning to stand on their own. The chicks watched the baby goats, bok-bokking their myriad questions, peppering their mother with them at a mile a minute. The ice cold sun was distant, but it was still showing bright through the force field and down upon all of them. It was glorious!

Sparkle sensed that what she was experiencing could in no way be real. She knew it was a dream, that her delight was due to Crosstown, but dang it if it wasn't a good dream. She felt the love she had for her children every bit as palpably as the shy sun on her upturned face. Sparkle glanced down at them and they gazed back at her, filled to the brim, simply overflowing, with love and trust. She felt their love. She felt it most intensely.

A shadow fell over them. Sparkle looked up and over where her shoulder would be if she had any and saw The Good Doctor, himself.

"Dr. Sir," greeted Sparkle.

"My Dear," he replied, kissing both her gobbles. He knelt down. The chicklings came to The Good Doctor and circled excitedly all around him. He smiled vast and let the youngsters hop on and jump about. Even when they accidently dropped bottom-bombs on The Good Doctor's crisp suit of clothes, he smiled and didn't mind. He knew the babies couldn't help themselves. They were immensely jazzed about seeing their father. The Good Doctor was not able to spend as much time as he would like with his chick-kids. They, of course, adored him even more because of this.

"How are all my babies doing today, hmm?" The chattering from the chicks became even more incessant.

"They are just beside themselves, husband," Sparkle answered for them. The Good Doctor laughed and smiled. Delighted, he stood.

"Follow me then," he replied. "I have something fabulous to show you all."

The chicks erupted, chirping, chattering and bottom-bombing the whole area.

"Wonderful! Children, everyone get in line and follow me. Chop-chop, now," she told them, "let us make haste."

The chicklings lined up and followed Sparkle and their father. The grown-ups led them through the gate and straight into the root garden where the gnomes dwelled. There was to be a ceremony today. They were all invited to attend the festivities.

A small contingent of gnomes was waiting for them, right between the rows of carrots and radishes. They all bowed severely at the waist when they saw their Creator. The leader of the gnomes prostrated himself before The Good Doctor.

"Rise, please," The Good Doctor stated and the gnomes all complied. The one who had prostrated himself turned and disappeared between the vegetable rows. The Good Doctor turned then to Sparkle and the kids and said: "They are wheeling him out now."

"Who is it?" asked Sparkle.

"It is one of their Elders. They are going to perform a ceremony of Renewal."

"What is that, my love?"

"Their eldest Seer is dying. The ceremony, the gnomes believe, will ensure that his wisdom, caring and strength remains with the clan."

The gnomes wheeled their Seer out on an old kid's skateboard. The gnome was tied down. He was still breathing, but just barely. Sparkle had the chicks back up a touch when some gnomes came forward. They all had wicked sharp spears. They rolled their dying leader to a stop. One of the spear-wielding gnomes came forward to the supine gnome. He bowed slightly from the waist and then plunged the spear tip into the chest and split the gnome open. He quickly cut out the heart, while it was still beating and squirting red life. He presented it to the reigning member of the Hunter Elite, who gobbled it down like it was so much pumpkin pie.

The eyes of the now dead gnome were popped out with the same spear tip. The optic nerves were severed and the orbs themselves were presented to the gnome's new Seer of the Clan. He ate the windows to the soul with relish and all due reverence. The wisdom that was necessary to lead the clan, the gnomes believed, were centered in the eyes. The brain of the former Seer was detached from the stem connecting it to the spine and presented whole to the Healer and Midwife to the clan. She wrapped it lovingly and took it with her. She was softly crying the whole time. Sparkle, The Good Doctor and their chicklings watched enraptured as the rest of the gnomes proceeded to empty out the thorax and abdomen of all the vital organs. They planned to cook it all in a stew for the whole of the clan to enjoy. Once they finished scooping out the dead gnome's still warm innards, the clan invited the chicklings to feast upon the remainder of the gnome. The gnomes wasted nothing.

The chicklings just adored gnome meat and the bones held much savory marrow. Sparkle smiled, delighted with the sight of the chicks gorging themselves. She was still smiling when the darkness closed around her and she was brought back up to the surface.

• • • •

SPARKLE WAS NO LONGER A MOTHER AND A WIFE. Now she was just Sparkle, the sex performer. Dang it!

Sparkle lifted her head from her deep breast and inhaled sharply. She came to, smiling at Donna.

"What do you think?" she asked Sparkle.

"That was really something," she said, trying to steady her excited heart.

"You liked it then?"

"Loved it," Sparkle replied. "I want in."

Donna grinned. This was more like it. "Excellent," she said. "How deep do you want to dive, Sparkle?"

The egg-layer paused a moment to reflect on her trip.

"All the way in," she replied. Sparkle reached into her clutch and removed the cash with her beak. She dropped the stack of cash she'd received for the solo performance into the waiting hand of 3D. "Fifteen thousand Rupees," she said. "Is that enough to make me an equal partner in this new venture?"

Donna looked down at the stack of cash. "Yes it will," she told Sparkle.

"Good," Sparkle replied, but with a catch. "Let me have a gram right now."

"No problem."

"And never let me run out," she added.

"You got it," Donna assured her. She smiled grandly at Sparkle. Another satisfied customer, the drug dealer thought. Sometimes it pays to get up in the morning. Even in this dirt hole.

●●●●

LOVE IS ALL YOU NEED.

It is a loaded gun and it shoots to kill. And even though it is a battlefield and it hurts, you need it, way down inside. It's a second-hand emotion and it's all you need. It burns when it's hot. It is a temple, the higher law. It can be deep inside, it can be suicide. It is a ghost train howling at the radio. It is the leech sucking you up. It is the vampire drinking your blood. It is like oxygen. It is like a dying ember, only memories remain. I want to know what it is. I want you to show me.

We only need the one more. Just one. Then We can skip the light fandango.

*Love is the key that fits a million locks. And We are going to find it.
Even if it the last thing We ever do.*
Love is all you need...love is all you need...love is all you need...

SEPTUM

SLOW BENNIE AWOKE IN THE USUAL FASHION. He opened his
eyes and tried with his feeble brain to determine his location. He
was fully clothed, lying on the floor of his bedroom. He had the
thumb of one hand lodged firmly in his mouth, suckling it. The
other hand was cupping protectively his penis and testicles. Slow
Bennie blinked himself awake as he remembered that he was
home. Then again, he was always home. Slow Bennie never went
anywhere off grounds. It was awfully cold up top and outside the
force field protected GRID.

Slow Bennie and his uncle Elron Hunt had to themselves
all of five hundred square meters of livable space underground,
which was good. Their home was certainly bigger than most. But
what was truly remarkable and valuable was the one-third of an
acre of GRID protected land directly above their domicile. This is
the kind of land that is worth more than can ever be quantified. Of
course Slow Bennie had no concept of this. He held no realization
of the immense value of his inheritance. He didn't know that that
was the main and really only reason why his uncle allowed him to
do whatever his punchy water head told him to do. Slow Bennie
just simply knew that Uncle Elron never ever punished him for
anything he did, no matter how stupid.

Fortunately for uncle and nephew alike, Bennie loved
being up top and Elron could care less. Bennie enjoyed tending to
the easier to grow fruits and vegetables that graced their table.
Elron was usually too smacked out of his mind to truly appreciate
the organic goodness the land provided. Feeling sorry for himself

and nodding his way into the loving and perpetually forgiving arms of Morpheus monopolized Elron's home life.

Beside the food bearing plants and trees, Bennie also had a knack for maintaining and shaping the pines and oaks and mulberry trees that graduated out in concentric circles from the fish freezer. Bennie loved his green time. It was his job and he took it seriously. The sowing and reaping and cleanup were delightful to Slow Bennie. The man-child had just enough going on upstairs to realize that the tiny farm (no animals; too difficult) was his job, while his Uncle Elron did his at the Club. Whatever the heck that was.

Slow Bennie liked farming, sure, but what he adored most was making fish jerky. He did it in the big dehydrator that came with the farm he had inherited from his dead mother, who had been a respected member of the Village Council. His Uncle knew how much he dug using the dehydrator, so Elron made sure to keep the freezer container well-stocked. This would keep Bennie busy and out of trouble. Well, most of the time, anyway. The frozen fish came from the handful of ice trawling clans that worked the perpetually frozen Lake and sold their wares at The Harbor Market. Elron would order the fish directly from the Market and someone would deliver it to the farm.

The dehydrator seemed to sooth Bennie and the jerked fish was spiced during the latter stages of the process. The smoked and dried fish was delicious, which is nice, because it represented the bulk of their animal protein. Most Harbor tunnel rats would never even see any animal protein except for the mutated rodents of which the denizens derived their derogatory name. The tumor-filled rat flesh kept them alive, anyway. The two of them were very fortunate and would be deemed quite prosperous by the standards of most. Even Elron agreed on the tastiness of Slow Bennie's fish, when he was sober enough to remember to eat. The fish were stored in a great big stainless steel lined box under a long shaft-like opening in the GRID. Responding to Bennie and Elron's verbal commands, as well as set on an automatic timing mechanism, the micro-pore openings in the GRID protected force field sent quick, tiny bursts of frigid ice age cold down through the long shaft before finding eventual solace in the freezer box. This kept the fish frozen until needed, without flash freezing everything else around it. It was still further shielded by a graduating outward ripple of tall boreal forest pines and other trees and shrubs and whatnot. This would keep most of the tiny bursts within those necessary confines. Bennie's mother did a fantastic job designing the small farm and Bennie had never known anything else. It was very pretty. He had no past to run away from or mourn, so he was happy and would be more than a little surprised to learn that not many other folks and freaks in the ACE Harbor shared his joy.

Slow Bennie rose from his bedroom floor, waving his arms and stomping his feet in an attempt to warm up some. He was already dressed in the same outfit he had worn all week, even the footwear. Bennie smelled horrible, naturally, but he didn't know this. He was one of those fortunate souls that enjoyed his own brand of funk. His Uncle Elron never complained about his nephew's malodorous cloud, so he had not the ability to even notice. Really, no personal grooming was ever discussed and Elron, unbeknownst to Bennie, avoided his bubble headed nephew like the Outbreak. He didn't like to brush his rotting teeth, either, and his Uncle never told him he should. So, the poor kid's choppers hurt him something awful, which is why he started the habit of helping himself to Elron's Downtown Leroy Brown whenever he could find it. The soft waxy plug liberally applied would numb his bleeding gums and after that, the slow swell of delight that builds within whenever he chewed it would make him forget his dental issues anyway. La, la-la. Even up top looked to Bennie as a brighter and even more beautiful version than it was of its own accord.

Bennie tore a pinch from his pinched stash and set it between the cheek and gum of the most painful area of his mouth. He could feel it working its opiate magic almost immediately. He intended to go up top and begin his farming chores, but he heard Uncle Elron returning home. The door from the thoroughfare tunnel access to the rear entry of their place opened and then closed just as quickly.

The man-child heard Elron come in and tramp his way down the short hall to his own room. Slow Bennie got himself even happier because now he had someone to play tricks on! If possible, this was maybe even more enjoyable than farming. He felt a wonderful butterfly tickle his tummy-tum and privates.

Boy, oh boy, this is gonna be great! He thought, excitedly.

Hearing Elron heading away from his bedroom, Slow Bennie ducked down behind his door. He sneaked a sneaky peek through the crack in his door at his Uncle's retreating backside. He saw Elron disappear into his bedroom and shut the door. He heard the lock as it was engaged and this made him giggle. Theirs was an old place and was never decked out with any thumb-print or eye-scanning locks. The doors were presently outfitted with good old-fashioned key locks and Bennie giggled into his hand because his Uncle didn't recognize that Bennie had a spare key. That was how he'd been helping himself to Elron's Downtown Leroy Brown. Silly Rabbit!

Slow Bennie snuck, as slowly and as carefully as his excited self could, down the hall to his Uncle's room. He stifled another giggle fit. The solar powered light above him turned on automatically as he passed beneath it. That won't do. Bennie was, after all, a Jedi, 007 super-spy, and a ninja all rolled into one. He crouched low and pretended to speak into his wrist, giving whispered instructions.

"Off," he whispered and the light was doused. He then went to the door and pressed his ear close. He heard a chop-chop-chop on the other side and lifted his pretend firearm to his chest, index finger pointing skyward, ready for action. Thank goodness that the fate of the free world was in Bennie's well-trained hands!

•   •   •   •

ELRON DROPPED HIS SHOULDER SATCHEL TO THE FLOOR of his bedroom. He kicked off his shoes and undid the tie to his drab shift. He padded in his thermal stocking feet to the desk, dropping the small zippie of Crosstown Traffic on the top. It was an unadorned, aged recovered school teacher's desk. Elron Hunt appreciated the simple small table. The uncomplicated metal and wood counter housed no lighted calendar, audio reminders, or any other technological doo-hicky-doos. Thank the blankety-blank stars above.

Elron was now as relaxed and at ease as he could get himself. He was going to go under once more and he made darn sure that he was only a short stumble back to his small awaiting bed. Elron was hoping to get ripped on a small bit of Crosstown Traffic and revisit his classroom again. He had loved the last trip so very much. But this time, the professor was going to visit his office with some company of the young, female variety. He was getting himself a rare Woodrow just thinking about it.

Elron crushed a little and sniffed it back. He began back-peddling just in time to tumble backward into the drug vision and onto his bed. Elron Hunt was unconscious and tripping stones before thumping the mattress. He settled back with a whimper and a grin.

•   •   •   •

SLOW BENNIE UNLOCKED HIS UNCLE'S BEDROOM DOOR. He carefully and quietly opened it and stepped with ninja stealth inside. His uncle was lying on his back, half-clothed on his bed. He was breathing kind of heavy and was pretty well red-faced. Bennie clocked the tears streaming down his uncle's cheeks and already soaking the bed sheets. Elron had a titanic erection and a blissful beam that belied the tears.

Slow Bennie laughed in his hand at his uncle's rigid tumescence and turned toward the desk. It was time to cadge some of Uncle's Downtown Leroy Brown. Imagine his surprise when he saw the small zippie of dried tears.

•   •   •   •

ELRON'S SECOND TRIP LED HIM FROM HIS CLASSROOM with a comely co-ed in tow. Laughing and flirting, Elron led his vision conquest to his spacious office at the University. He unlocked the door and opened it wide, beckoning the young lass inside.

She took care of shutting the door herself, and locking it tight. The down like a clown, Charlie Brown, frosh was on her knees in a freeze-framed instant. She began squeezing and pulling on Elron's pud like it was a nearly empty soap dispenser. The professor had his hands in her brick red hair, watching her felate him with more skill than any nineteen year old should possess. He could feel her warm mouth and wondered with much anticipation what exact shade of ruby her tulip was going to be, when she morphed right before his eyes.

• • • •

SLOW BENNIE SAW HIS UNCLE'S MOUTH OPEN and close as his eyes fluttered and lolled beneath the lids. Even in his softened brain, Bennie knew the small pile on the desk was goodie good goods.

He went to it feverishly. Slow Bennie intended on gobbling the lot of it.

• • • •

"BENNIE!" SHOUTED ELRON WHEN HE SAW WHO was on his knees with his mouth inexplicably wrapped tight around his constituent. He shoved at his nephew out of sheer outrage, and none too gently either. "What do you think you're doing? Where the heck is Cammy?"

But Bennie didn't say a word. He shook off his uncle's attempt at force as though an insect had landed. He clamped down even tighter on Elron's and then bit the head completely off, blood squirting everywhere. Elron screamed, feeling the pain acutely and real as a counterpoint to the pleasure and wet warmth. He punched at his nephew viciously, fully expecting the lad to reel backwards, but it did not transpire. Instead, Bennie suckled even more uncomfortably his uncle's associate as though he was trying to drain him dry. The boy was trying his level best to empty the man standing before him. Elron was boxing his nephew's ears and ripping handfuls of hair from the handi's head. Slow Bennie kept at it, though, ignoring his uncle's violent assault and verbal abuse.

It was very much like his life depended on leaching out every tiny liquid jeweled drop of Elron Hunt's precious fluids.

And nothing was going to stop Us.

••••

YES, THIS IS SO MUCH THE BETTER. ELRON IS DRIPPING now so delightfully and seems to be on the dreadful verge of expiring. Not to worry, he has served his purpose and has served Us very well.

The next phase is essential and is made possible because We have complete control of this puppet We inhabit. His name is Slow Bennie. His mind is weak and he now belongs to Us. Delightful. And as a collective merging into One, the thoughts and voices and needs have become MINE. Everyone's opinions are controlled now by the singular Self inside this lone Slow Bennie shell. I am I and I can do what I will.

The fish dehydrator is inspired. I can regain from Elron Hunt so much that has been diluted and lost. I will drink him dry, drink as much as I can stomach, as much as I can digest. It is a homecoming of sorts. Then, after I am done with him, I shall need to get some more.

With the knowledge of Elron Hunt and the power of our rejoining, I know just where I have to go. I have become self-actualized and whole. Therefore, I know exactly what I need to do. I don't know why I am and where I originated, but I'm going to find out everything. I swear to you I will.

I shall go backwards…

OCTO

MY SLOW BENNIE BELLY IS UNCOMFORTABLY FULL of Elron Hunt's juices and bits. Much too distended for me to have enjoyed my very first bicycle taxi ride through The Harbor's underground tunnel system. It was such a strange combination of sensations, too. I mean, on the one hand, the blood bounced around in Slow Bennie's gut. The pain and urgent desire to vomit was horrible. However, every minute that I was able to keep it all down, the clearer everything became. The stronger and more in control I became of his body movements and reflexes. And, despite the fact that I, Crosstown Traffic, am still in my infancy as a sentient being within this water-headed meat puppet, I know just where to go and just what I need to do. It is much like opening up a book, one with all the right answers splayed out before me with no explanation required. Almost like downloading information and knowledge all at once. It is a heady feeling.

And when all is done that must be done, I will still remain the young human male: Slow Bennie. Which means that I am the sole heir to a quite nice piece of GRID protected Harbor property. Slow Bennie was unable to conceive what that meant on his own. I know he never realized how important and valuable his sanctuary was. Uncle Elron did, I could certainly ascertain that from ingesting him, but he was far too troubled to take full advantage of it. But, hey, that's no problem anymore, because I certainly do. Slow Bennie's home will make a safe and comfortable launch pad for all my gnarly deeds manifested via my wicked, wicked ways. So, beyond the need to belch, void and defecate, things couldn't be going better for yours truly, thank you very much!

The bicycle taxi came to a halt at the address I gave the Halfling taxi driver. I had liberated Uncle Elron's money purse before venturing forth, so I had cab fare at the ready. I stepped out of the open carriage and dropped – I wouldn't touch the lizard claw – into his ... whatever that thing he (she? it?) was holding out. The driver smiled, I think, and dipped the head in thanks. I was making my way toward the entrance to the Club when I had an inspiration. I turned back.

"Say – uh – Buddy, how can I get a hold of you on the quick?" I asked.

He (I'm leaning heavily toward male, now) stuck out a long gecko's tongue and licked his left bulbous eyeball. He said: "Just tell the door-man to call Randall on your way out. I will be here in less than five long ticks."

"Thank you," I replied, surprised at how civilized scale-boy was. "I'll do just that. And the quicker you do get here," I added, flashing Elron's stack of Rupees, "the more of these you'll earn. Dig?"

"Yes, Sir," Randall replied. He then climbed back on to the seat, kicked his tail out of the way, and began pedaling. He merged effortlessly into the phalanx of the funky and freaky that seemed to never really thin out.

I entered the Balmy Breezes through some dry ice like vapor and paid an exceedingly stiff cover price to a diseased looking bouncer-type. He stamped Bennie's hand and let me in through a thick, smelly wall of fish and chips, smoke and stale vagina. I liked it immediately.

The seat I chose was at a table that was closer to the bar than the stage. I planted my anus on the plastic chair, reveling in the wonderful newness of it all. I glanced around, noting the other patrons and what they were doing. As I've said, as soon as I saw things, they made perfect sense to me. It was like I just needed a catalyst to get me going. The other patrons were alternating looks between the stage in the distance and the small touch-screens imbedded in the tables before them. They seemed to all have their cash stacked on the table, and were using the screens to make their choices. Pussy on tap. How very convenient.

I placed my cash on the table top and peered at the screen. Apparently tonight was "Headliner/Amateur" night. The professionals were on the main stage, hence the steep cover, while the amateurs would work the lap-dance loop through the raucous bar crowd. There were plenty to choose from as far as lap-dancers went. The screen had pages of them. I was still gazing at the choices of women, boys, Halflings and whatnot when a server approached my table.

"Good evening," she said with a smile that was only missing a few teeth. Speaking of which, Bennie's were starting to pain up something awful. I might have to get them all pulled soon. I'll start over with some implants, like the ones Uncle Elron had. Anyway, the server asked what was my pleasure.

"Are you running any specials tonight?" I asked with a big rotten toothy Bennie smile. The server glanced over her shoulder. She leaned in to me.

"Sugar, I can get you a gram of Uptown Girl, a lap dance of your choice and two double Sterno Ethanols for only two hundred Rupees. You pay me up front."

"Sounds good, Love," I replied and grabbed her hand.

"Hey!" she began with a shout and a grimace of pain.

I tugged her roughly down to me, "I may look nice, sweetheart, I may seem to you like a mark, but I assure you, I'm not."

"Ow, okay," she said. She gazed into Bennie's eyes and saw me. She believed. "Okay," she repeated, understanding my intent.

"I'll give you the whole two bills," I said, "and you are going to bring me what you promised. Tout suite, gorgeous." She just nodded, took the cash, and walked away rubbing her wrist.

I chuckled, feeling better now, and succeeding in forgetting Bennie's dental woes for the time being. I looked at the screen at the available dancers. There was only the one choice for me: the red one. The screen said she would be available in a little bit.

The main stage got nice and dark and the server brought back my gram and cocktails. They were ice cold and on the rocks. You know, ice not being too hard to come by. She set them all down and as she turned with a pout to leave, I slipped a fifty note in her waistband. She stopped, fearfully, but smiled when she saw the nice tip.

"However," I told her, "I do have my moments."

The server left just as the music began to swell and the stage got lit. I decided to join it and slugged back the first drink in three big grimace-inducing gulps. I dumped the gram right onto the table top. I could hear the Headliner taking the stage as I rolled up a Rupee note and stuck it in the white pile. I snorted up as much as I could, as fast as I could, then tipped my index finger into the second cocktail. I sopped up most of the remaining powder, rubbing and numbing it liberally over Bennie's choppers.

I looked up, sipping the second fire-water, much slower, getting ready to settle in and start the real plan. I was looking for her; the one that's next. The dope was kicking though and the drink was softening my gaze, and that's when my lap dance arrived and I was distracted anew. I do believe that red is my favorite color.

The Halfling sidled up to my lap and placed a gentle hand on Bennie's shoulder. I could feel her heat. She smiled seductively, really without even trying. She licked her fangs with her pink, forked tongue. Her red devil's skin was both hide and silk. Her horns were short and sharp.

The demon Halfling danced slowly to the rhythm of Bennie's pounding heart. She leaned in close and gently rubbed her hot face against Bennie's warming one. And when she did, the trigger compressed again. I felt something there, faintly stirring beneath her skin. A memory; a series of them.

It made me inhale sharply and snap reverse against my chair back. She stared at me, clearly confused at the turnabout. I was obviously into her, but now I must have seemed almost frightened. Admittedly, I was a bit disturbed, but more excited than fearful. She didn't understand. She stared at me, deep inside Slow Bennie, trying to figure it out.

"Do you want me to leave?" she asked.

"Oh, no," I replied, thinking how odd to run into someone here that knows Him. She knows Him, the one I ultimately want. This beautiful Halfling knows the Creator.

And she knows where He lay…

"Please," I say, smiling, turning back on the charm. I stand quickly and pull out a chair for the darling girl. She knows Him. I spotted the server nearby and called her back over. "Whatever this beauty wants," I say, serious as a heart attack, "she gets."

"Of course, sugar," she said to me. She raised her thoroughly pierced eyebrows at the dancer. "What'll it be, honey? The Special?"

The dancer nodded and I gave the server four big notes. "For the both of us," I added.

I handed to the dancer the remainder of my drink. She sipped at it while a gamely scraped the grains and remains of Uptown residue together to fashion for her a halfway decent line. She smiled at me and snorted it up, pinching her nose adorably afterwards.

"Thank you," she replied with her little tinkling of a voice. "You are very generous. Do you want me to finish your dance now?"

"You are most lovely," I admitted, easily enough in that it was true blue, but: "I'd rather enjoy your company instead, if you don't mind," I said and peeled off another hundred. I placed it beside her and she retrieved it with another one of her killer smiles. "Perhaps you wouldn't mind terribly sitting and talking with me for a bit? Maybe answer a few questions?"

"Sure," she said, "that's fine." I smiled back at her.

The server returned with our Specials. I gave to her another one of Elron's fifty notes and she got the message and left without a word. Good girl, that one. I took a sip.

"Do you mind if we get high first?" she asked.

"By all means," I said, "That's a first-rate idea, young Miss."

We spilled out our grams on the table and bent right to it. I pulled up, feeling the Uptown Girl in all its glory. I leaned back, rubbed some more on Bennie's receding gum line. I picked up the Sterno Ethanol, jiggling the ice chunks. They tasted like they were gouged right out of the Lake, but I was feeling way too good to care about such trifles.

I turned to look at the dancer. I asked her, "Do you know who makes this stuff?" indicating the Uptown. "Do you know how it's done?"

"Sure," she replied, "Don't you know? It's no secret." I didn't answer that, I just kept on smiling at her, waiting for her to spill the beans. "Everyone knows him. He is a great man," she finished, somewhat wistful.

"I don't doubt it," I concurred. It was good gear. "But, who is he?"

"He is The Good Doctor," she replied. "He is The Harbor King."

"Excellent," I said. I'd hate for him to be just some clever schlump. I thought a moment, "Do you know where I can find him?"

The dancer just smiled at me.

Damnation Beneath The Frozen Apocalypse

• • • •

I FINISHED THE REST OF MY GRAM, the dancer having moved on. I'd given her another hundred and the whole expensive diversion was well worth the cost. She'd told me many things. They were wonderfully detailed things about conjoined twins and a private lab. About the hospital the Creator ran and the all-important Damnation Scores. She explained that the very best drugs came from the ear wax and the dandruff of the twins. The rumors about the salt from their tears and the brand spanking new narcotic it produced. She told me their names, all of them. I then knew how I came to be, that it was the pile Slow Bennie gobbled up in his Uncle Elron's room, and his before that, and so on and so forth, all the way back. It all became very clear to me. I understood the compulsion to consume the previous users. That was what I tried to gather unto to me, it really was I, my essence. The urge, now that I know, is even stronger. It was all very fascinating and enlightening information that, I swear to you, I intend to put to good use.

I sat back, contented and thinking long and hard about it all. I sipped the gut bomb and absently watched the main stage as the next Headliner prepared to make her entrance.

It was a grand one at that. The jolt it gave me made Bennie sit straight up. There she was. I mean, this is why I came here, but it was still a marvelous joggle. The next one in line going backwards was there Headlining on the main stage. I should have known she would be a pro. I had wanted to eat her just like I did Uncle Elron, but it changed everything seeing her in the flesh. She had me inside her. I craved to go back in and not just to retrieve more of myself. There was much more to it than that. So, I just stopped right there, in the name of Love.

What, I ask you, are the odds?

My plans changed on the spot.

NOVEM

I HAD RANDALL FOLLOW THE HEADLINER FROM THE CLUB. He (I'm most positive, now, he's a he) traveled down the tunnel, away from the Club, as she made her way home. I sat back and tried to stay my excitement by glancing around. There wasn't much to see down here. There's just the usual blend of the far-out and crazy – crazy in how they look, crazy in how they behave. Crazy. This place was in want of a killing spree. Maybe later.

My Bennie's heart was hammering like mad and I was almost dizzier than I could stand. Randall was doing a fairly decent job of keeping her taxi in his line of sight. The nice length of sharp cutlery was still satisfyingly heavy. It was strapped to Bennie's calf, hidden as it was beneath Uncle Elron's ridiculous shapeless shift.

I was going to gut her. Or, perhaps I was going to cut out her still beating heart and squeeze the hot blood into my open, waiting mouth. I was. But not now. Not anymore. Instead, I have decided that I'd much rather ask her to be my Valentine.

Don't you think that'd be sweet?

• • • •

DONNA HAD A BAD FEELING THAT SHE WAS BEING FOLLOWED. The tunnels can breed that sort of paranoia. 3D chuckled to herself. She hoped it was only paranoia. She recalled an old hospital saying from before the C.E. : You're not paranoid if they really are out to get you. Too true, that.

Regardless, she could not shake the feeling of someone, or something gaining on her. It was horrible. 3D even considered taking the long way and looping all the way around the giant underground circle instead of simply pulling into her garage, which was right up ahead. Once there, she could lock herself inside, but something nagged her not to do this. Donna listened to the fearing nag. She passed her casa and looped herself around.

It would prove a regretful decision.

• • • •

RANDALL SLOWED AS SHE MADE IT TO HER STOP UNHARMED. I put my hand on his shoulder and ducked down a little lower behind it.

"Hold still for a minute," I told him. I watched as Sparkle got out of her taxi. The doorman for her complex (pretty nice digs…) held the door for her and she went inside. "How am I going to get in there?" I mumbled to myself.

Randall heard me and he replied: "Why, that's easy, Sir."

"How's that?" I asked.

"Because the Doorman's a Downtowner, Sir."

I just stared at him as he slid out of the seat. He adjusted his tail and made his way over. I could see Randall talking to the doorman. Cash (mine) was exchanged. He nodded to me and that was my cue.

I was in her building in two shakes. Finding her flat should have proved the most troubling of all, but she housed a part of me inside her already. I didn't know then if she could feel me, but I sure could sense her. It was strong and drew me as a moth to a flame. I was on her door step and knocking, just like any legitimate gentleman caller or upscale customer. I was neither and when she opened the door, I shoved her inside. I locked the door on the quick.

Sparkle back-pedaled, hitting a key table or something, and fell over. I felt bad. I tried to make amends and to make Sparkle feel safe. She wasn't having any of it.

"I'm not here to hurt you," I tried to explain.

"What do you want, then?" she frightfully asked me.

"To love you," I replied.

• • • •

THE TUNNELS WERE FULL. Humans and Halflings alike were everywhere. Half of those lived there and the other half were just visiting or passing through. The tunnel system itself was shaped more or less like the jagged spokes on a worn down to the nub wagon wheel. There were fair to middling sized recesses and big enough alcoves in every corner. These dark and dank corners were where no sane being would want to be caught alone. That's where she found herself.

The poor thing.

The tunnel rats were congesting these out of the way inky spots. They were a moveable congregation of sustenance, teeth and hunger. They were in all places and the tunnel rats represented both ends of the food chain simultaneously. Their over-sized eyes glowed fiercely in the dark as they scavenged those that had expired, or at least those of whom could not outrun the pack swarms. The tunnel rats bred rapidly and in large numbers, making them the shrimp of the A.C.E. subterranean world. The rats kept scores and scores of folks alive. When the pups were flash-fried, they popped similar to kettle corn. The older and meatier ones tasted just like chicken.

Donna wasn't thinking of mock chicken fajitas, or tunnel shrimp, or any of that. She just ran with a panic and without thinking, straight into the all-enveloping darkness. She ended up in an alcove that was a one-way blind. She had a large pack of tunnel rats snapping at her heels. When she turned around, she could see their glowing eyes. A light-show that bit, tasted, scrambled up her legs. The rats gnawed on her as though they'd never tasted flesh before. Their instinct was feral and all-consuming. Donna didn't like that; not one bit.

Donna looked scared when I grabbed her. She was kicking and screaming, raining ineffective blows upon me. She was quite out of her head by this time, the poor thing. Sparkle couldn't drive, having nothing but ornamental stumpy wings with useless, miniscule digits at the end, but she made a nice look-out. Neither one of us could tell if it was us, or the tunnel rats that were hanging off her like bats on cattle, that was freaking her out so. From the car lights that could just barely penetrate far enough for me to make her out, pitiable Donna was lit-up and glowing with green rat eyes and her own red blood. She was a spitting image of a Christmas tree in Satan's recreation room.

It could have been us that frightened her. My bet would have to be on the tunnel rats.

While Sparkle waited by Donna's car, I came wading in to the alcove. I was kicking and stomping the tunnel rats with wild abandon. Finally, enough of them were killed or injured, so that the horde's attention was on the pathway of least resistance, which was to turn tail on their own kind. The tunnel rats dragged off the dead and dying. They went fiercely to a safe, darkened recess around a corner away from us. I picked Donna up off the ground, peeled off the remaining furry leeches and flung her over my shoulder like a fifty kilogram sack of potatoes. She did nothing to resist, so it was dead weight I was carrying. Bennie's body is very strong and the car door was open. I tossed her in, Sparkle hopped in and I got behind the wheel. I pulled quickly into the stream of slow traffic while Donna kept thanking me, over and over.

It was like she thought I was rescuing her, or something. Huh.

••••

SO, I HAD HER GAGGED AND HANGING UPSIDE DOWN. We were in her flat and she was suspended by her ankles. I had bound her wrists tightly behind her back. She was doing lazy, hazy, crazy half-circles above a big, empty punch bowl. When I slit her throat, she bled out in under a minute.

By this time the two of us understood one another. I was in love, certainly. I don't know if she was with me. It didn't matter, because we two were joined and she accepted the inevitability of it all. She gobbled up Donna's spilled blood as quickly as I had consumed Uncle Elron's. I did have some of Donna's blood myself, of course. It was necessary in order to further join Sparkle and to enhance ever further our unholy alliance. The Headliner consumed the vast bulk of it, whilst I de-boned 3D's carcass. I needed a suit to get past the eye–dent.

We both snorted some more of the twins' potent tears. We then had some wild, bizarre sex that did not transport us anywhere, it seemed. It did, however, make time bend and twist on us. Hours had passed that began to feel like whole days. It was enchanting in and of itself, but we both felt it was still a distraction. We had the occasion, but it seemed to us that pursuing sexual gratification was squandering the gift of time. We were wasting it on mere amusements. There was still more work to be done.

The de-boned carcass of Donna would fit, if I stretched it taut enough, like a suit over the body of Slow Bennie. Ingesting her gave both Sparkle and me the directions to the big farm.

We made our way out of Donna's flat and to her car. I had on the carcass suit, wearing it as a hooded cloak. When we get near, I'll tug it down over my face so that her dead eyes would register and we would be let in. I hoped.

I so wanted to meet the Creator. I longed to speak to him. I need to see where he lived and how he lived. Then? Well, then I am going to kill him. Don't you see? How many chances does one get to kill their god? I don't know, but I will only need the one.

Don't you dare judge me.

••••

UNCLE TUGMUNKEE WAS PUT OUT. He was ready to seize a little time for himself when the visitors announced their arrival. The Good Doctor was up top, out in the gardens, amusing himself. It was Tug's nap time. He'd already cleared his schedule with The Good Doctor and he planned on taking a trip with a line or two of Crosstown Traffic. But now someone was at the door.

"Bother!" Tug exclaimed. He sighed deep, resignedly and chimp-knuckled his irritated way over to an adjacent wall-screen. "Who's there?" he asked, doing nothing to disguise his aggravation. The screen lit up with the eye-dent of The Good Doctor's niece and Sparkle, the sex performer. "Open the line," Tug ordered the screen. "What the heck do they want?" to himself.

###

The Good Doctor was up top in the gardens. He had just teleported home to the farm from Hell's Mouth. He still had on his travel slippers and his 9s were still strapped. The Good Doctor strolled leisurely about, Billy on his heels like an overgrown, hoofed puppy. He absently scratched Billy's chinny-chin-chin and hummed softly to himself. He pulled the silver gun from its holster and placed it in his mouth. The Good Doctor fired a blast of Uptown Girl down the back of his throat. He held the persuasive spray for a long count. He exhaled slowly after holstering the weapon. The Good Doctor grabbed a waiting Billy by the ears.

"Not enough, I need more," he said. The Good Doctor dragged the silver 9 out again and repeated the ritual. "Nothing seems to satisfy," he mumbled, the sprint concentrating. Billy sat back on his haunches and waited for the Creator to draw it out. "To breathe, to feel, to know I'm alive..." When he did, Billy sucked and nibbled at it until The Good Doctor's expulsion covered his goat-face. Billy licked his goatee clean. "Thank you, Billy," The Good doctor replied and asked the goat-guy to check in on the gnomes. They had been ill of late. The Good Doctor was understandably concerned. The Devil's in the details.

• • • •

AT FIFTEEN MILES PER HOUR IT TOOK FOREVER to get to the farm. The upside being that Sparkle and I were able to get good and topped up on Uptown. We drove toward the center where the underground entrance to the farm waited for us.

Sparkle obliged me while I drove. Bennie's left hand was on the steering wheel and his right I'd thrust right up her tiny little stink-hole. I could feel an egg forming. I crushed the shell inside her, making her twitch and moan. I dragged out the slimy mess and spread it like marmalade on my stick. I would have forced her to eat it all, but she did it on her own.

I love her with all my heart.

• • • •

WE CAME TO THE UNDERGROUND ENTRANCE TO THE FARM. I yanked down Donna's face, hiding my eyes behind Bennie's, behind hers. The eye-dent scanned all of ours, including Sparkle's.

So far, so good.

• • • •

"WHAT DO THEY WANT?"

"Doctor, Sir, they say there has been problems with Crosstown Traffic. There's been some serious complaints."

"What sort of complaints? Violence?"

"Yes, that's what they are saying, but they are refusing to elaborate," Tug told The Good Doctor. "Donna and Sparkle will speak only to you, Good Sir."

The Good Doctor thought a moment.

"Very well, Tug," he replied. "Send them up."

• • • •

BILLY HEARD THE COMMOTION FROM INSIDE THE CONFINES of the root garden, where the gnomes dwelled. There is danger lurking and it is dreadfully nearby. He snuck to the very edge of a hedgerow. He peered carefully around the corner.

• • • •

SPARKLE WAS OUTSIDE DONNA'S CAR when Uncle Tugmunkee opened the inside door. We had already pulled into the garage and parked. I'd slunk low, very low down in the front seat as the garage door slid shut behind me. Only Donna's head that I wore as a hat showed above the dashboard. Tug held the door for Sparkle. When the chimp's back was turned, I slipped quickly and quietly out. Taking unfair advantage of Tug's being a gentleman, despite being a chimp, I came up on him hard and fast as he let Sparkle hop up the stairs. I'd shucked the Donna cloak as I ran at him. He turned and was too startled. Tug could not react in time to get inside and secure-lock the door. I knew, gentleman or no, how strong chimpanzees were. I put the point of my blade under his chin. I pushed him into the domicile, applying enough wicked pressure to puncture his thick hide. I got Tug off balance enough to force him in the interior. Sparkle shut the door with her beak as soon as the chimp was in. I spun around and got behind him, pushing all the while up on the blade. By merely touching the bald chimp I knew he was also in on the Crosstown Traffic gang. And knowing that meant Sparkle and I will be having chimp for supper tonight.

But first things first.

"The Good Doctor, please," I said, hauling him deeper into the residence, trying to keep the bastard tilted. Heaven help me if Uncle Tugmunkee got his feet firmly planted. I had to show him who's boss, so I traced the blade along his jaw line, opening him up a touch. He winced and I put the point back where I had it.

"What do you want?" he asked and I bore down on the blade, digging in ever deeper.

"I already told you what I wanted." Imagine that; the early work trying to out-smart the opus.
Cheeky.

"Okay, then who are you?" he asked, before foolishly adding; "No need to introduce her. I have met this whore on previous occasions."

I cuffed the chimp in the right kidney, hard.

"Say you're sorry to my True Love, or I will peel the flesh from your bones, monkey."

"I apologize," Tug wisely and immediately replied. He was wincing from the pain. The chimp will pee blood before this day has concluded.

"Where is he?" I reiterated. I dug the knife in a bit deeper, for good measure.

"Up top," Tug replied.

"Show me," I ordered. He did so.

• • • •

BILLY CAME SLOWLY, CAREFULLY FORWARD. He couldn't figure out all the details and consequences of the play that was acting out before him in the courtyard. But he, like all of The Good Doctor's creations, was hard wired to shield the scientist from harm. The nice chicken lady and the blood-drenched man he'd never seen before seemed to Billy as though they meant severe damage.

Billy was bothered because he had never in his life felt fear from The Good Doctor. Billy must do what he had to save him.

Closer now…

• • • •

THE GOOD DOCTOR SENSED THEM, BEFORE HE SAW THEM. Almost as if the Mighty One had whispered in his ear, he turned hauling out the black 20 shot nine mm. He had it pointing deadly at us. He stepped forward, frowning all the way.

"By all means, keep coming, Father," I told him, wrenching fiercely on Tug. "If you want your manservant bled, that is."

He stopped, no doubt noting Tug in pain and the sheen of blood that was drip-dropping down his bare chimp chest.

"What's the meaning of this?" he asked, still pointing the gun. I decided to duck down, hiding myself behind Tug's squat body. If the Creator wanted to take a shot at his creation, he was going to have to shoot through Tug to get to me.

"You don't recognize me, Father?" I asked him.

"I have never seen you before, young man," he replied, cocking his head and eyeing me quizzically. "Why do you refer to me as Father? A show of respect, perhaps?"

"A literal representation, Father," I explained. "I am the manifestation of the tears."

"Tears?" he wondered. Then he smiled. The Good Doctor said: "'I beheld the wretch – the miserable monster whom I had created'," he paused then added, "Of course, the tears."

"You seem to have put it all together," I commented, "and in short order, too." The Good Doctor was a genius.

Sparkle stood nearby, staring fixedly at The Good Doctor. My Creator, my Nemesis.

"Just look at him, will you," my True Love mumbled this nonsense.

"What?" I said. Perhaps I didn't hear Sparkle plainly. Perhaps... "What did you say?"

Without even looking at me she replied: "Oh, shut up. I wasn't talking to you."

And just like that, I was yesterday's news. She wasn't talking to me, or looking at me. The Good Doctor smiled at her and smirked at me. I got mad at that, I did. Sparkle just cooed. I got distracted. I was going to get them both, but out of nowhere, I got hit from behind. I flew through the air, ass over tea kettle.

Sparkle wasn't talking to me...

Uncle Tugmunkee's throat got slit as the intruder flew through the air. Billy had the presence of mind to use the same horns that head-butted Slow Bennie to nudge and push the chimp toward The Good Doctor. Sparkle ran over to him on her own accord. She began rubbing herself unabashedly and moaning.

The Good Doctor knelt beside Tug, staunching the chimp's free flow of blood. The knife wound was deep and painful, but it was nowhere near fatal.

"We need to move," The Good Doctor stated.

"Why, my darling?" asked Sparkle.

The intruder shakily got to his feet. He looked as angry as one could get, seeing his True Love jump ship at the drop of a hat.

"That's why," The Good Doctor replied. They all glanced over at Slow Bennie. He grunted something wild and unnatural; guttural. He began stomping over to the group. He had the bloody knife pointing toward them and was following it rather quickly. Slow Bennie looked dangerous and determined. "Can you move, Tug?"

"Yes, Dr. Sir," Tug replied, standing fast.

"Good. Then let's get behind the retaining wall as fast as we can manage."

They started moving, but so did Bennie. And he was gaining on them quickly.

Tug, Billy, Sparkle and The Good Doctor hid behind a wall. They could hear Slow Bennie moving closer. He sounded furious and way beyond any point of reason. Tug and Billy were with it enough to be frightened, but Sparkle did nothing to help out except for making moon eyes of obvious love at The Good Doctor, who, fortunately for all concerned, had the presence of mind to order the force-field to flash-freeze the intruder.

After the frigid blast had dissipated enough to keep from doing the old gentleman any severe damage, The Good Doctor came out from behind the wall. The rest of them peeked around the edge, or over the top of the barrier. The Good Doctor began firing. He emptied the entire 20 shot clip into Slow Bennie.

Satan laughing spreads his wings…

And that was all she wrote for me.

It was the goat that did it to me. It came out of nowhere, taking unfair advantage of my disturbance and commotion, knocking me down. Then, from my unfortunate seated position, I had the distinct displeasure of seeing my One and Only drop me for the Father like a bad habit. Oh, well. I am nothing if not resilient. Time for some good old-fashioned righteous retribution.

I stand, spitting out some anger and venom. I start stomping toward them. They ran, all of them, from me. Instead of heading toward the house and some semblance of real safety, they opted to hide behind a vine-encrusted wall. Now, why would they go and do something foolish like that?

I heard Father shout out something about an intruder, me presumably, and then I froze; dead in my tracks.

I knew nothing, no more. Mine was the shortest life in the history of ever. Well, well, why don't you look at me, huh? Just falling to pieces.

Ridiculous.

"Juggling is sometimes called the art of controlling patterns, controlling patterns in time and space."

–RONALD GRAHAM

ACTA EST FABULA

IT'S ALL ABOUT KEEPING ALL THE BALLS IN THE AIR. Not every person can do it, but it is a skill that is crucial. By gum, if you are going to be a despot, be a good one. Juggle, baby! Do it like your fool life depends on it.

When I am born this final time, my Father holds me while Mother cracks open my egg. Father pulls apart the shell and Mother eats the placenta I am encased in. I am born fully aware, both of my surroundings and of myself. I know who I am, what I am and where I come from. I am The Monster in its final incarnation of Crosstown Traffic. I am the tears of the twins, fully realized.

I'm not quite certain if Father and Mother realize what I am. I do know that The Good Doctor and Sparkle are my parents and that they will both love me, their child; down to their last dying breath.

I look like a perfect melding of them both. I have feathers mixed with hair instead of only hair. They are pretty much in the same locations on my person as you would find anyone's hair. I know Mother will have them twisted together, when they grow out. She will fashion silver-black feather sprouted dread-locks. You will have never seen the likes, trust me.

My eyes are quite human but they are over-large. These eyes rest a little bit closer to my recessed ears than my all-human counterparts. My eyes move independently of each other. I can see in more than one direction, so don't ever try and sneak up on me son…can't be done.

I have human lips stretched over an upper and lower beak which replaces the need for human teeth. I can snap off your fingers without issue. I will have to learn to be extremely careful with my sensitive human tongue. I'm an omnivore. I can and will eat anything and thrive on it all.

In close to a decade, when I am fully grown, I will top out around one and a half meters, but barrel-chested and weighing in at over 90 kilograms. I will walk upright and will be as quick as the dickens. I have small, but fully functional arms and hands. My fingers and thumbs (2 on my left, like Father) are webbed, as are my feet. I house claws instead of fingernails and toenails, with the obvious advantages therein. My IQ shall be hard to measure. My temper, I can already tell, still wet as I am from birth and Mother's ministrations, is quick and unpredictable.

I am The Good Doctor's finest creation and an only child. The only one that will live, that is. I will see to that.

I am an Antichrist like my Father and I am his Monster.

I know that, without any doubts whatsoever, that Father and Mother will be wonderful parents. They will love me unconditionally. They will guide me and teach to me all that they can. They will provide all that I need to grow and thrive here in the harsh and unforgiving environs of The Harbor in the A.C.E world. I already love them for it. I love them even more than my fully matured self will be able to adequately say. I look forward to growing and flourishing under their combined tutelage.

I come from the tears that were quite real. Those that I will shed shall also be genuine. As factual as I am. I will be truly saddened on that forthcoming day. I will allow myself little regret, just sadness as I kill Mother and Father. And then I will eat them both.

I will possess all of their knowledge and all of their wisdom. I will inherit all of The Good Doctor's wealth, which is good. You know, one less thing.

I am an Antichrist like my Father and I am The Monster. But I can Juggle, man. I can Juggle like a motherfucker.

...AD FINEM

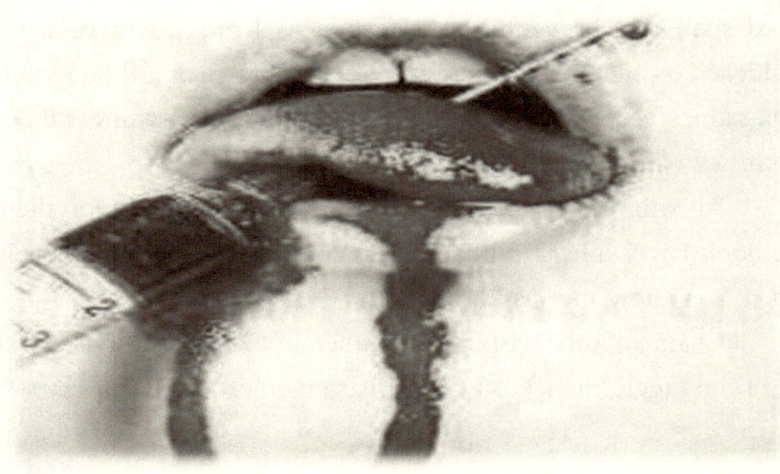

BLOOD AND BUBBLEGUM

"Have a care; I will work at your destruction, nor finish until I desolate your heart, so that you shall curse the hour of your birth."

~The Monster
–MARY W. SHELLEY

BUBBLEGUM WAS TRUSSED UP PRETTY LIKE a nicely glazed holiday ham. She was an egg-layer in her late teens, a good bleeder, and lay on the examination bed. They were deep in the bowels of Hell's Mouth Determining Hospital, far below where the real patients rested.

The Nocturne eyed her closely, savoring the sight and smell of her. He was the hombre de la hora and he was dying to get a taste of her. She was moaning softly, pulling oxygen in and waiting for them to give Bubblegum her snacks. She gyrated gently against her soft restraints.

"More," she softly pleaded, "Make all the bad go away."

The Good Doctor was on the other side of the subterranean exam room, nodding his head at her. She'll get what's coming to her, no worries. There are proper procedures to follow, my beaked beauty. There are no short cuts in good medicine. The Good Doctor pulled off his floor-length lab coat and wrapped it around a wire coat hanger. He loosened his tie, undid his shirt. The Good Doctor kicked off his loafers, unbuckling his belt as he walked toward Trudge and Drudge. He followed his huge, pharmaceutically enhanced erection. The conjoined twins stared out of three eyes, at some unknown subject at some unknown distance. The eyes were all the same washed out, milky-white, baby blues. The Good Doctor stopped in front of their cage, were they sat mewling and drooling out of their two mouths and sloppy down their one chin. He discarded the remainder of his outfit and slipped on a lovely gold sequined ball gown. He tied back his salt and pepper dreadlocks, tugged up his gown and stuck his pecker into Trudge's mouth. Drudge's over-sized tongue lapped sidewise at it. The Good Doctor took a silver pen casing and scratched at the dandruff on the twins' aircraft carrier of a melded cranium. Their sparse hair coated with Uptown. He pushed and shoved the mostly white dandruff powder into a tiny pile. The Good Doctor bent at the waist and snorted it up. He put his head back inadvertently popping his cock out of Trudge's suckling toothless mouth. The Uptown hit The Good Doctor like a Bolivian Bullet Train, lighting him up. He disappointed the twins when he stepped away. They had mistakenly thought it was dinner time. It was not. The Good Doctor's ejaculation was being reserved for his sweet little furry pussy cat. He'll get someone else to feed Trudge and Drudge. He stuck an index finger into Drudge's ear. He retrieved a golden brown gold-piece, which smeared evenly and all around his fingertip.

The Good Doctor went back to where Bubblegum lay and Pilate waited with Juan and Mary. He sat a plush divan, close enough to get a good view to a kill. The Good Doctor whistled low and a tabby patterned cat came flouncing in. She came up to The Good Doctor, jumped up on his lap. The cat was a bit smaller than the average house cat. It was made from the DNA co-mingling of feline, monkey and The Good Doctor's own dead wife. Sweet little furry pussy cat had an extra-long thick tail with a functional gripping appendage at the end. The tail mimicked a tree-swinging monkey's, used for both gripping and for balance. The cat had a long, lithe body with finger indentions that match The Good Doctor's grip perfectly. The face of the special clone had the whiskers and fur of a cat. But with human eyes of stunning emerald and the full, plump lips of The Good Doctor's long lost loved one. Her lips peeled back to reveal sharp, feral teeth, but with a thick, flat and wide pink human tongue. The back of the cat's throat had tonsils. Once you get past those, your cock would then be massaged by the cat's gastro-intestinal tract which was the exact DNA image construct of the widower's dead wife's juicy twat. The inside temperature was an exact 38 degrees. The extra warmth was like kissing sunshine.

The Good Doctor tore a new little peek-a-boo in his gown and took out his rock steady. His cat put her mouth right on it and began lapping away at his cream dispenser. The Good Doctor gripped his pussy. He stroked himself while the kitty purred.

"Now this motherfucker knows how to party!"

"Get to it," The Good Doctor ordered Mary, who stood right next to Bubblegum. "Let's get this train rolling," he stated. He moved kitty-kitty, bang-bang, up and down while he chewed on the Plata wax on his fingertip, getting that Uptown/Downtown cocktail just right.

Bubblegum's eyes fluttered. Her dark lashes were moist, her beak slightly chapped and clacking; the breath sweet. Her talons stretched and clenched, her feather trail wet from wanting. She was beautiful. The hep-lock plunged into a vein in the back of her spine was new and bank. You could see it pulsing.

Mary tapped out bubbles and shot the girl into another world.

"Oh, blessed lord," she moaned. When the Plata hit her hardest, her mumbling ceased and the whites of her eyes glowed, the pupils hidden, staring at herself. She turned rigid, flushed. Bubblegum was rushing her little balls off.

"What does she look like inside?"

Juan, hearing this second outburst, glances over to the corner, by the twins' cage. Morbid stood there. His long, lank hair obscured most of his face and what you could see of it was covered with the wet shit from whence he came.

"I bet it's so pretty in there," mumbled Morbid.

"Fuck," Juan muttered as low as he can. He doesn't think anyone in this exam room could see his own personal Jesus. Nonetheless, Morbid's timing was as rotten as usual. "Get back in here!" Juan mouthed at the shaking, red-eyeballed man, standing and dripping foulness onto the stark white floor.

"Oh, all right," Morbid pouted and began to slog his way over to where Juan already had his chinos tugged down to his ankles. He pulled apart his butt cheeks. Juan looked irritated over

his shoulder at Morbid. The fuck was taking his sweet-ass time with it. Juan kept glaring at Morbid until he finally got over there. Juan, squatting, prepared for the pressure and Morbid seeing no chance at being allowed to stay out, parted the rectum of his provider and crawled up and in. Juan stood, gritting his teeth. He zipped up his pants and buttoned them just as Morbid settled down.

"You never let me have any fun."

"Shut the fuck up, you," Juan admonished. "Now stifle yourself. I want to watch this." He turned back to the girl.

The girl's breathing quickened, her skin turning bright red with the swell of oxygen pounding her shores.

Pilate smiled, then. He showed clearly teeth that lengthened as the grin spread wicked across his pale cold face. His eyes lit up all yellow and beastie-boy.

"Take her," Mary told the Nocturne. She walked back to where her man, Juan stood. The Good Doctor was getting himself all lathered up. "She is all yours now."

He bent to her. She was down for it, slick saucy and sweet.

For a moment, Pilate lost himself.

The blood, he thought, was sipping paradise.

)O(

Juan and Mary knew that Pilate was a Nocturne and they were smart enough to be afraid. Even still, they were dying to meet him. He had it all and they wanted in.

The couple sat in the bar sipping cocktails, just as they had done every evening for almost two weeks straight. They watched him appear. Just appear, man, right out of thin air over by the bartender.

The vampire handed the nigga a package which vanished beneath the bar top in an instant. It was exactly the same routine as the last three times. It wasn't a pattern, exactly, not one that could be fingered, but they knew he would eventually show up because the dealer always did. He had to deliver his drugs. Juan and Mary knew if they were patient and waited long enough, Pilate would show.

The small, tightly wrapped package should be Plata if they knew their guy, which they did. The bartender, Steel Ovid, handed Pilate an envelope; cash, most certainly.

Pilate peered inside the envelope, checked the denominations, gauging the thickness. He didn't count it though. The Nocturne didn't need to. No one in their right mind would be stupid enough to buttfuck the drug dealing vampire. Even so, he looked like he could use the help of a couple of down motherfuckers like Juan and Mary. You know, to help with the day to day. The young couple just needed a way in.

Pilate looked at Steel Ovid. He said something to him that Juan couldn't begin to hear across the distance of the bar and the slow, deep throb of the hardcore gangsta shit blasting forth from the DJ's station nearby. Whatever it was must've scared the god-fuck outta the dude, cuz he stepped back and put his hands up in surrender and fear. The bartender backed up a quick two-step as Pilate leaned in, his long tightly curling hair spilling in a wave, obscuring his face. The menace in the gesture and what he must have said was full and uncomfortable like a dildo on a church pew. Steel Ovid looked frightened bad, dropping his arms and folding his hands. He lowered his head, nodding in supplication, staring at his feet. His quaking Juan could see even from across the room. The nigga was a big dude, too, really more imposing than even the vampire.

Steel Ovid was a huge, heavily muscled albino. He had orange corn rows and was festooned with homemade prison ink. Professional tattoos displayed his fight wins. They were all over the place. He was a big and scary motherfucker who had a reputation for immense, visceral violence and the hair-triggered temper to go with it. Folks were scared of Steel Ovid as if he was a blood-drinker himself. But the poor, scared fuck was not and the nigga threatening him was.

"My God," Mary said, watching the scene with Juan, "You ever see that big fucker scared before?"

"Steel Ovid, no way," he replied, "Never. It's interesting though."

"For sure," she spoke, took a quick sip of her cocktail. "We sure are looking at the right dealer to hook up with, that's clear." Juan nodded his agreement, noting how Pilate stood straight and then in one quick movement, turned to look right at him.

"Fuck," spat Juan, his own fear bursting within. That nigga's eyes were yellow and backlit. They looked like a night hunting panther's, glowing as they were at Juan.

Then, just like that, he disappeared. Juan turned quick to Mary. She was still glancing that way. He opened his mouth to speak and saw the color vanish from her face. Her lips quivered and her eyes grew wide. She then backed up and Juan turned to see.

"Fuck me!"

And there Pilate was, standing right in front of Juan and Mary's table. Speechless, they stared at the vampire and he right back. And then, without a single word, Pilate dissolved on the spot, gone without a trace. There was some displacement of air, a slight cold whoosh and that was it.

It was a few moments before Juan and Mary could breathe and the bartender, they could see, was even more fucked up by his encounter than they. From where they were perched, they could see the Steel Ovid shaking like he had wet hair in a meat locker. He turned to the racks of liquor behind him, ignoring customers coming up. He poured himself three big shots of top shelf tequila, slugging them one after the other. When finished, he pinched the bridge of his nose, shut tight his eyes, leaned on the ledge running below the bottles. He collected himself with a final big breath and straightened up. Steel Ovid went back to work just as the Authorities came in to the bar.

The Occupying Indian Army made their way slowly through the bar. They were just making their presence known, being sure to stay away from the rooms in the back. The rooms in the back led down stairways to the bathrooms and other dangerous locales. The patrons hid any activity that was overtly illegal, but were otherwise left unmolested and to their own demise.

"Wonder what Pilate said to him," Mary mused as several soldiers passed. She shook her lonely ice cubes at a passing barmaid and was ignored. "Just when I really need one, you bitch!" she yelled after and was still shunned. The Army Captain looked back at her. Mary just smiled at him, as sweetly as she could manage.

"Shit, girl," Juan told her, "have mine."

Juan handed her his mostly full drink. He was right. Mary knew she shouldn't be drawing any attention their way. She shut her trap and threw the drink back. The Indian officer turned and kept moving away.

"Jesus, who knows what he said," he muttered, thinking, getting them back on track. "I mean, shit, baby, motherfucker didn't say even a word to us and I feel like climbing into a hole and pulling the earth in after me."

"Exactly," she agreed. "Whatcha think, Papi, should we just forget it?"

Juan wondered that very good point for a moment. Then he said: "He sure is scary, for real," he told her, "but he's our way in." Mary nodded in agreement. "And once we are in," Juan continued, "We won't have to be afraid of anyone else, baby. Not in the whole of The Harbor."

"We'd be the big-dick daddies, for sure."

"Yeah," he agreed, "If he doesn't kill us first."

"Still," she said, "It's clear he needs our help."

Mary pushed Juan's now empty glass away and reached into her purse. She pulled out and lit a thin, pre-rolled blunt of half tobacco and half homegrown Mary Jane.

"She's my main thang..."

"He really shouldn't even be here," Juan mused, "it's not safe."

Mary pulled hard on the blunt and nodded.

"Shorties or even the two of us should be flippin' shit, not the top dog."

"That's for sure," she said, handing Juan the blunt. "How are we gonna hook him, though?" she asked.

Juan smoked and thought. He knocked ash on the already very dirty bar floor. "I was thinking of an offering." Mary looked at him closely. "A gift," he said.

"I don't know," she responded, taking back the blunt. "I mean, just giving the motherfucker a sandwich won't do it," she countered, "He can hunt whomever he wants, true?"

"Yeah, but he's exposed and shouldn't be."

"Also true," Mary agreed. "Oh, shit, wait," she said, looking back to the bar. "There's our answer."

Juan turned to where she was looking and saw a young comely Plata fiend. The egg-layer moved slow and sexy through the crowd, touching many patrons, speaking slow with a naughty tongue lick of her beak. On and on she went, clucking down the bar, looking for a daddy.

Juan smiled at Mary's idea. They looked at each other.

"But if we gave him the gift that keeps giving…." trailed Juan.

"We will need some cheese for the trap, baby," Mary added, gesturing toward the now recovered bartender. "And I know where we can get it."

Juan sucked on the blunt again, held it in. He loosed out a big plume and handed it back to Mary.

"Go and scoop her up," Juan told her. "Ply the little coop-chick with drinks and a few lines. She doesn't look like she shoots up."

"No she doesn't," Mary agreed, "At least not yet." It was impossible to tell that from where they sat, though. What with her little bent wings tucked up against her large succulent white meat breasts. She carried a small bejeweled clutch tight to her body.

"Yeah," Juan nodded, seeing where she was going. "Now you'll get to use some of your long dormant paramedical training, get her set up for the long haul."

"Think she'll go for it?" Mary asked, watching her get rejected and looking more and more anxious." Egg-layers weren't everyone's cup of orange pekoe, apparently.

Juan stood to let Mary out of their booth. "Does it really matter?" he asked. "Little baby Bubblegum over there looks like she'd fuck herself with a pool cue for a taste of the Silver and we're gonna keep her fucked up on Plata 'round the motherfuckin' clock."

"And if she doesn't go for it?" Mary insisted. Bubblegum's feathers were bright shiny silver and hard black. She kept them plucked so that all of her pay parts were covered. She had a big plume of whispery feathers, reminiscent of hair, as a cloud halo crown. Mary thought she was sexy as fuck. She knew the vampire would dig her, that's for sure.

Juan smiled down at Mary. He thought Bubblegum was sexy, too. He said: "I think blood taken by force will taste just as good as blood given. Don't you, my love?"

"Yes I do, you fucking gorgeous creep," she replied, biting her lower lip, nostrils flaring. Juan knew she was getting wet. Maybe Pilate would let them play some too.

"And me. Don't forget your little butt-dwelling buddy, Morbid. She looks good enough to eat."

Ignoring Morbid, Juan bent down quick to give Mary a kiss. Her breath caught as he probed her mouth with his teeth and tongue, finally ending the kiss with a nippy ball of spittle which he launched down her throat.

"Go fetch," he ordered.

She swallowed and smiled.

Mary went to the bar. Bubblegum was leaning against some older dude, trying to laugh at his lame shit. The guy had the biggest set of salt and pepper dreadlocks she had ever seen on a pasty-face. His suit was immaculate. He did not look like he belonged in this shoddy watering hole, but he had that expression on his face that fairly shouted: "Slummin!"

Keeping half an eye on punkin' pie there, Mary got the bartender's attention, while purposefully ignoring fancy dreadlocks' stare.

"Two Crown rocks," she told Steel Ovid, placing the empty glasses on the bar top and pulled out some cash. She laid money down for the drinks. The motherfucker will know what Mary wants when he sees the flash of cash. Paper money sales were always frowned upon these days. The Occupying Indian provisional government preferred patrons to use their very traceable digital accounts, bar-coded to a micro-chip under each legal citizen's left wrist. Transactions using paper Rupees or the Federal Reserve Bank Trade Notes that the International United States – who's terra firma The Harbor physically resides upon – is condoned, but just barely. The standard exchange is a 2 for 1, making the insistent cash holder lose money. But when one is purchasing narcotics, well... Everyone looks the other way.

When the barman served up her drinks, Mary smiled sweetly, wrote on a bar napkin.

"My phone number," she told him, loud enough to be heard by anyone giving a shit. She handed over the napkin to the bartender. Steel Ovid picked it up and looked at it closely. He saw the two bills folded inside. He looked up at her, Mary smiling sweetly.

"I see a 2 here at the end of your digits....that right?"

Mary nodded, "Uh huh."

She straightened and waited for the barman to make change. She turned slightly, saw the girl losing interest. Dreadlocks seemed to actually think she wanted another drink. Bubblegum was getting increasingly anxious, no doubt her Plata high was wearing off and she was at the very beginning edges of panic. Bubblegum's head was doing the herkie chicken jerk. She was unable to keep her head from bobbing like she was seizing. Mary could see the cluck was ripe for plucking. Mary got her attention. The old man turned away from them both.

"What's your favorite color?" she asked the girl. The bartender turned back and gave Mary her overly lumpy change and her cocktails.

"What's that?" Bubblegum asked, turning full to her.

Mary smiled back at her while counting her change. It was all there: two 5K NewRupee notes, two 1Ks and a small zip-locked baggie holding two grams of thick gummy ear wax Plata. She let her new friend see the taut little yum-yum bag.

"I asked you, what's your favorite color?" Mary repeated, "Silver, right?"

"Yeah, new best friend," Bubblegum clucked, "Plata is my favorite color."

"Well then." Mary replied with a growing knowing smile, "Come with me and I will make all your dreams come true." Bubblegum immediately left the bar, following Mary without a moment's hesitation.

)O(

JUAN WENT BACK TO THE SAME DARK SHODDY BAR, AGAIN. And, again, he went without Mary. She stayed away to tend to Bubblegum, keeping her stoned and happy. The comely coop-chick still thought they both had a sex crush on her. They let that cluck-fuck fantasy remain intact.

"I wanna shove it up her tiny stink-hole."

Juan needed to find Pilate, this time, for a face-to-face meeting. Nobody knew the vampire, or where he cribbed or how to contact him. It didn't matter, however. Juan wanted no one but his Mary and him in on this plan. The Harbor may be a post-industrialized ghetto shit hole, but they knew small town rules still applied. Everybody knew everybody's business: who was zoomin' who. It's just like Mayberry, but with a much higher body count. Except in Mayberry, Andy and Barney wouldn't let you get the skin flayed off your body while fucking a dead dog for a 5K NewRupee auto-deduct.

"Fuckin' squares!"

They could tell no one; trust no one. One word of what they were planning and niggas might kill them simply because they hadn't thought of approaching the vampire Plata dealer first. Once again, Juan made his way through the drunk and fucked-up bar crowd. He was nervous as all hell. He'd been drinking more than he should, smoking super-strong ghetto weed constantly. Finally, after almost two weeks of this nerve-wracking shit, Mary pleasantly surprised him with a handful of muscle relaxing pills which he doled out to himself; one at a time. It helped a great deal as he trolled the same sleezy, sticky, loser filled bar, night after fucking night, waiting for Pilate. He was worried the blood-drinker wouldn't show up and even more nervous that he might. Juan did a perfunctory head check of the patrons, seeing no Pilate around, had to pee. With some growing dismay, he pushed back, deep into the bar, toward the back hallways, stairs and the toilets.

Juan split the curtains of human skin, replete with freckle, scar and mole stains, and pierces the confines of That. He entered the first hallway. Juan took the stairway down, following the signs to the bathrooms. Humans and Halflings alike were engaged in all manners of drug consumption and sexual congress. A young girl was tugging on folks, pleading with them all for the return of her hymen. Juan just shook his head. How the fuck should he knows where her freshness seal is? Shit.

"Shit!"

Juan stepped down about six more feet before he came to the first body. The male was long dead, judging by the smell. But that didn't give the old woman with a bald, spotted scalp the right to straddle his below the knee leg amputation. She periodically coughed up mucous from her blow hole onto her hand. The old woman used it to further lubricate the dead fuck's stitched, blunted stump-cock. As Juan carefully and quietly passed her by, he noticed she was vaguely see-through.

"We gotta go through Hell's Own asshole, just to take a piss?"

Ignoring Morbid patter; --"Hello?"-- Juan kept working his way down in to the dark red smoke, until he finally reached the landing. There he saw a man with his hands secure-tied behind him. A taut, tight rope of aborted fetuses pulled up the man's wrists. The babies were secured to each other by their own long, convoluted umbilical cords. A sulfur and sugar smelling pit-demon was feeding the rope of abortions through a dog skull pulley. The man's mouth was buried on a firebrand. The acrid smoke curled from his burning mouth. The demon stared hard at Juan whilst he pulled on the rope. He dislocated the man's shoulders and kept pulling. The man never made a sound. Only his tears bore witness to his True Pain.

"Can I go to school here? It looks like they got some Level 10 pain downtown, Bubbie!"

The restroom was filthy and crowded thick with men pissing. Trannies were sucking dick, their johns holding cash above their bobbing head as a promise. Drugs were being snorted, deals going down. Some nigga was desperate enough to tie his shit off in this horrid crapper in one of the door-less stalls, flicking up a vein, trying to feel for a bump to target his needle.

"Gross."

Juan went into one of these stalls. Some passed out fuck, pockets having already been turned out, slumped over to the side, head planted into the feces smeared wall. He considered trying to wake him or dragging him off the seat. Instead, it was most expedient to simply pull out his pecker and piss on the motherfucker. He wouldn't care.

Juan was just shaking it and zipping up when he sensed someone. He looked up and right into the face of the old man with the big mass of dreadlocks again. The same polished slummin' dude that was trying to holler at their Bubblegum. He smiled cruelly at Juan. His jumpy nerves made him cringe.

"You sure you want this, dear fellow?" asked mister fancy dreads.

"Want what?" Juan retorted, confused. The old guy is human, not a vampire, not a demon. That means dreadlocks teleported himself here. Other than the Indian Army, Juan had never meant anyone who could afford teleporting. He figured if someone teleports themselves into this shithole, Juan had better pay attention to what dreads was saying. At least dreads didn't have to go back up through all that shit to get to the bar again. Juan would.

"Are you sure you want to meet the blood drinker?" he asked Juan.

"What's it to you?" Juan wanted to know, getting wide with the cunt out of a deep-seeded need to not kowtow. It was ingrained and had gotten Juan into trouble many times.

"Don't get smart with me, young man," he admonished. "I am The Good Doctor," he began. "I am Pilate's sponsor and protector. You need to be sure of what you wish for."

"Why's that?" Juan asked, a bit more politely.

"Because it may just come true," The Good Doctor stated. And then he winked out.

Just then a cold hand dropped solidly on to Juan's shoulder from behind. It was strong. The talons growing out of the split fingertips dimpled Juan's coat, punctured the cloth, and pressed into his flesh. Juan was surprised at how much it hurt. He sucked it up though and stood tall.

"When you wish upon a star..."

"You got balls hunting me," the Nocturne told him. Pilate squeezed a little more and made Juan hurt a lot. "But do you have the heart?"

"Makes no nervermind who you be..."

"I'm not after you, we mean you no harm."

"What do you want then?"

"We wanted to meet you," Juan told him.

"You and the girl you were with?"

"That's right. I was hoping to speak with you."

"And you are?" the vampire asked with a bit more pressure. It was getting bad, the pain, but Juan knew a test when he felt one. Juan told him their names and intentions. "Services?" he asked, "What services?"

"Whatever you need, you know, help," said Juan, arm going numb, fingertips tingling unpleasantly.

"You two want to help me sell drugs?"

"Yes, exactly," Juan replied

"And what, exactly," Pilate mockingly replied, "makes you think I won't kill your uninvited ass where you stand?"

"Because we would not dare to seek you out empty handed, Sire," Juan told him.

"Stop the ass-licking sire shit, I don't like it," Pilate warned, "And it will not help to keep you, or your Mary alive."

"What shall we call you then?"

"Nothing yet," he said. "What do you have for me?"

"We have an offering."

"Offering? What kind of offering?"

"Blood," Juan stated," "A continuous stream of it."

The Nocturne smiled then. "Yes," he replied, "That might do."

"I can take you to Mary, where she is being kept for you. And then we can bring her to where you stay."

"And this token of your esteem is in hopes that you and Mary can work for me, with me? Is that right?"

"Yes, exactly," Juan agreed. "We can be of great value and help. We can assist and protect you."

"What do you hope to gain and I expect the truth from you," Pilate advised with one more, tiny squeeze, "Your life, where you stand, depends on it."

Juan did not have to think, Mary and his motivations had never changed. "We want in," he said simply, "And you are the way."

"The Truth shall set you free."

The vampire was silent as he removed his painfully frigid grip from Juan's shoulder, blood seeping now from the talon punctures. Juan could feel him moving close to whisper in his ear.

"Well now, seeing as you two now work for me," the vampire said, "I guess you should call me Pilate."

We're in, thought Juan.

We are!

)0(

BUBBLEGUM WAS BROUGHT INTO THE EXAMINATION room of Hell's Mouth Determining Hospital, via the back. She didn't fight them a bit as she was led down an old, rickety elevator. They dropped loudly down several floors, far below the main floor. Pilate and The Good Doctor were waiting for them there.

He had no family, friends or associates to lookout for him. Beyond The Good Doctor, Pilate had no familiars or anyone to help him with his work or to keep him protected and safe. He had no underlings. Now he does.

His almost complete lack of social graces attested to his lonely life.

But his new employees, Pilate's new friends, were here now and they did not come to him empty handed. They had brought such a gift.

The pressurized intravenous line ran from the metal IV stand next to the girl's bed, to the jugular vein in her pretty neck. A 3-way stop-cock kept Bubblegum's precious blood from squirting all over the aseptic, stark white floor. Heparin and saline filled the taut IV bag and kept the blood from clotting and dying. The teenaged egg-laying girl had an oxygen mask on her face-beak, a big green metal tank standing tall in the corner.

For a Nocturne, it was the best kind of breakfast in bed. Juan and Mary stood nearby, excited and happy. The Good Doctor sat forward, working his hand-held pussy cat in quick, smooth-pulling tugs.

Pilate went to Bubblegum and knelt at her side. Juan and Mary watched their new boss and benefactor. The blood drinker turned to get permission from his sponsor.

"Get her," The Good Doctor told Pilate.

And that was it. They had done it, they were in.

They smiled and held hands as Pilate opened the stop-cock and began to feed. He was making everyone's dreams come true. Bubblegum was quivering now. Her blood being siphoned by the vampire, she moaned and cooed and bok-bok-bokked until her big breast and plump thighs were a writhing and wriggling mass. The feather trail that went between her over-sized dark meat thighs dripped her come. An egg shot out of Bubblegum and skittered spinning across the floor. It came to a stop at Juan's feet.

"Let me have it."

Juan looked to Mary beside him.

"Go ahead," she whispered, "Let the freak have it."

"You heard her," Juan replied in his matching whisper.

"About fucking time," Morbid replied. He poked his pressed fingertips through Juan's rectum, making his meat puppet pain out a little. No big deal. He slipped his hand down Juan's chinos to below the cuff, and grabbed Bubblegum's egg off the floor. Morbid slid it back up the pant leg and inside Juan's ass in a second. Juan's ass made a small flatulent that he had to clear his throat with a cough to cover. Morbid's muffled chewing of the shell and slurping of the ovum inside was a gurgle storm from Juan's abdomen. *"That's more like it, fuck-tard,"* Morbid told him as Bubblegum caught her breath and The Good Doctor's sweet pussy-fur lost hers, *"But I'm still gonna gut her."*

For fuck's sake.

....END

Also available from ~MorbidbookS~
In Print & Kindle Editions. Available at Amazon.com,
WWW.MORBIDBOOKS.WORDPRESS.COM
and Barnes&Noble online.
~click on following cover images for HYPERLINK~

~ **It wasn't long before the contents of his mysterious** trunk were revealed to her. It was true, they were props, and some of them might even have been used in the circus. Whips and crops, handcuffs, gags and blindfolds. He applied each of them to her liberally and with sadistic abandon. She took to each of them and craved more. This was the other side of Salero, the one he hid, the dark side. Publically, the man loved and craved the laughter and applause of children. But as much as he craved the laughter of children, he also craved the cries and screams of women as they submitted to his own particular brand of sadism. He wielded a whip better than any lion tamer in the business. It thrilled him to watch the firm young flesh of a woman writhe and twist in delicious agony as his ropes bit deeply into them and his crops left myriads of latticework markings on their bodies. Their anguish was his delight.

~**Rae is her name.** Our support group of embittered and most likely deranged women are going to kidnap, torture, disembowel and finally kill the woman who has ruined all our lives. As foul and as grotesque as she is, she acts like she's Queen of the Bean. Rae, her buck-tooth grin and rosy cheeks of middle age acne reflected winter sun. Straw-like blonde hair obscured by the veil and tiara she enjoyed parading around in. She walked past our window with sickening confidence oblivious to us and our weak tea. Rae. Everything was always about Rae. Was she a princess today, or was she a bride? We wished we could be that delusional and walk around with an air of not giving a damn. Rae believes she is above the pain she has caused. Beyond the whimpering of her victims. Out of reach of vengeance. Our support group of women do not agree. Judgement day is here for Rae.

~Maybe it had started when he was at university.
He had a girlfriend in his final year that had gotten him into some weird stuff sexually then she left him for a guy with a bigger cock. The other guy was some gay looking chump with muscles and a tattoo; the pair had died in a car accident and Brian took a dump on their graves after each of their funerals. Fuck the both of them. But after she had left him he needed to fill the void of the newfound enjoyment of sickening sexual practices. Brain had purchased one of those 'real life' sex dolls online. Boy did the thing look real; you could bend it into any position and it came armed with enormous tits, willing mouth and a supposedly real feel pussy and anus. The packaging said to 'just add lubricant' but there was a problem. There was something missing; the smells, the tastes and the feel of real skin. You can't emulate that. So Brian set out to attempt to build a real life sex toy made from real life people.

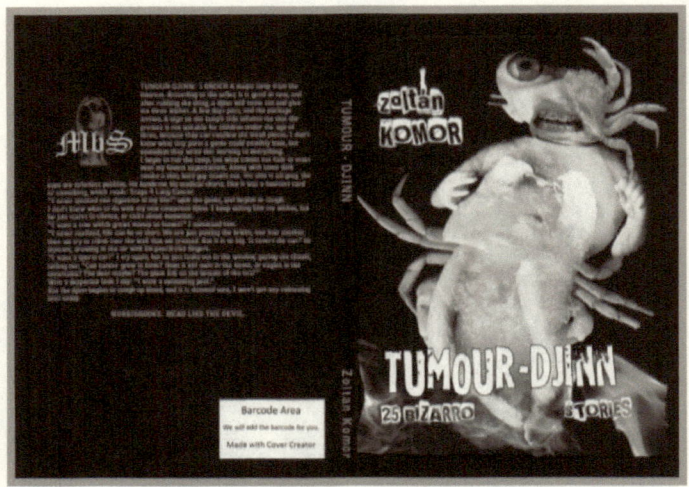

~I ORDER A magic lamp from the internet. According to the seller, it is good as new, and after rubbing the thing, a djinn will come out and give me three wishes. I begin to rub the lamp. Along with some dark smoke a thin, bald guy crawls out. His skin is all grey, the eyes are colorless pebbles.

"I want a tree which grows money as leaves!" I command.

"I never realized life can be so short. We are just putting the bricks, one into another, and then we try to climb over the wall that we created. But it is so big. It covers the sun." he mutters.

"I want a sports car!" I try again, but he just looks out in the window, gazing the clouds, telling me: "Can cancer grow in birds? Does it kill owls in the forest, or eagles in the mountains? The deer maybe? The giant fish on the bottom of the sea?"

With a desperate look I say: "I want a swimming pool."

But the djinn begins to cough up blood, and it is damned sure, I won't get any swimming pool today.

~**Keegan is a late-night public access radio show host,** sexual deviant, and militant vegan. He has grown tired of his vegan cause being treated with apathy by the portly, meat-gorging, residents of the small town of Breen Gay, Wisconsin.

The time is ripe for Vegan vengeance.

Keegan harvests roundworms from a local vagrant and mutates them using chemicals stolen from the meat packing plant. He infests the populace with the voracious, parasitic carnivores. Keegan knows that the only way for the people of Breen Gay to eliminate the parasites is to starve them of meat.

It is with great expectation that he awaits the oncoming utopia of Veganism.

However, the mutant roundworms will not die easily. The problems for the people of Breen Gay have only just begun.

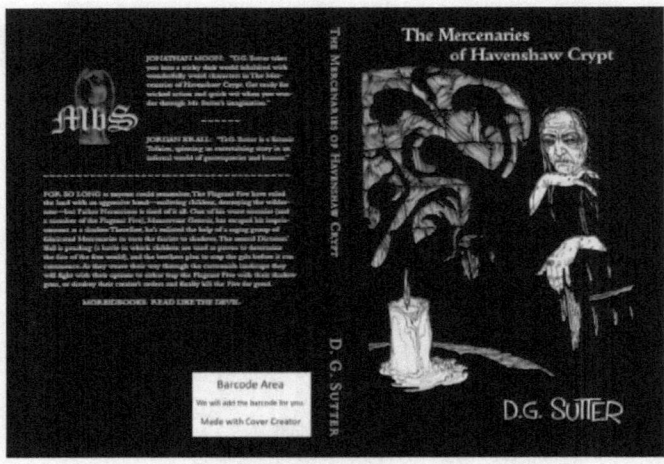

~For so long as anyone could remember, The Flagrant Five have ruled the land with an aggressive hand—enslaving children, destroying the wilderness—but Father Necrocious is tired of it all. One of his worst enemies (and a member of the Flagrant Five), Manservant Genesis, has escaped his imprisonment as a shadow. Therefore, he's enlisted the help of a ragtag group of fabricated Mercenaries to turn the fascists to shadows. The annual Dictators' Ball is pending (a battle in which children are used as pawns to determine the fate of the free world), and the brothers plan to stop the gala before it can commence. As they weave their way through the cartoonish landscape they will fight with their options to either trap the Flagrant Five with their shadow guns, or disobey their creator's orders and finally kill the Five for good.

~The hands of the girls were inside of each-others zip front grey boiler suits and they sat in the blood from where Sonny's face collided with the surface. The brunette had a finger smear of it next to her mouth.

"You two sluts put each other down and go tell Moira that Sonny's done. I'm coming in, just got a little business to attend to first."

As the two started to leave the big blond grabbed the shoulder of the red head and pulled her back.

"Not you Fire-Crotch, all this fucking blood has got me going." She started to unbuckle the belt on her camouflage hot pants. "Down you go, bitch!"

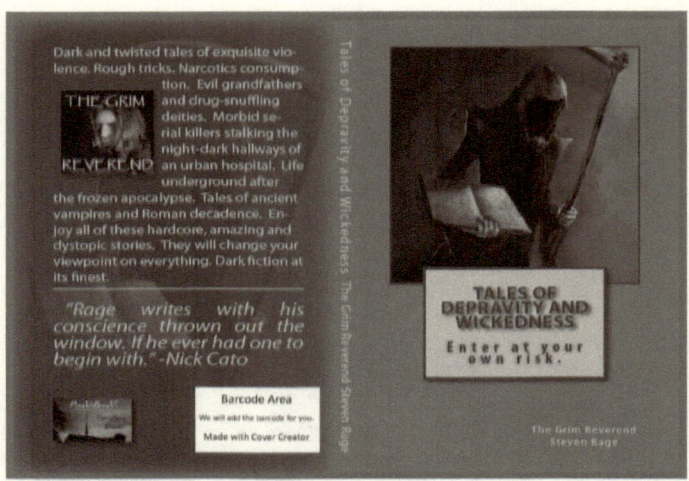

~**Short stories from the Most Depraved Writer in Print.** Dark and twisted tales of exquisite violence, rough tricks, narcotics consumption, evil ghosts and drug-snuffling demons. Evil grandfathers and animal–human hybrid clones. Morbid serial killer stalking night darkened hallways of an unsuspecting hospital. Life underground following the frozen apocalypse. Tales of ancient blood-thirsty vampires and Roman decadence. Enjoy all of the hardcore, dystopic, viscerally violent stories. Not for easily offended mamby-pambies. Dark fiction at its finest.

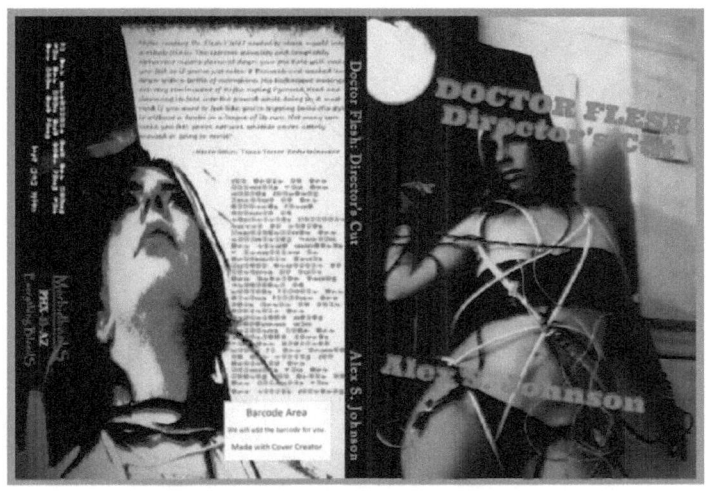

~From Alex S. Johnson, the author of Bad Sunset, Wicked Candy and The Death Jazz, comes a new vision in Bizarro horror. Imagine a TROMA film on meth and acid, one part cyberpunk, one part Franz Kafka, and three parts frankly unsuitable for a sane audience. "Will make you feel as if you've just eaten 8 Percocets and washed 'em down with a bottle of moonshine," says Necro Stein of Texas Terror Entertainment.

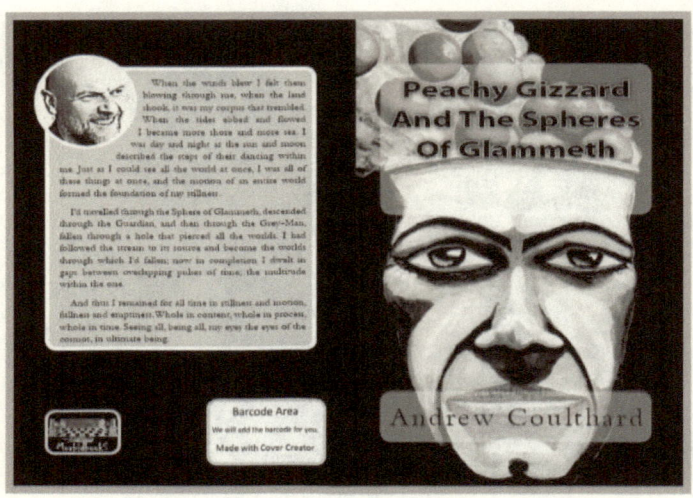

~When the winds blew i felt them blowing through me,
when the land shook, it was my corpus that trembled. When
the tides ebbed and flowed I became more shore and more
sea. I was day and night as the sun and moon described the
steps of their dancing within me. Just as I could see all the
world at once, I was all of these things at once, and the
motion of an entire world formed the foundation of my
stillness.
I'd travelled through the Sphere of Glammeth, descended
through the Guardian, and then through the Grey-Man,
fallen through a hole that pierced all the worlds.

~He had to have her the moment he saw her trachea ring. Six months later she was his lovely wife. He performed his duties as a husband and she as a wife. He tolerated a house filled with references to her late first husband and the children they had together. He put up with her prudish ways. He waited. He was patient. He planned. He was adaptable. He was rewarded over the course of a week in her basement. He turned his perverse sexual fantasies of worms and maggots and her lovely crusty trachea ring into a gruesome reality.

~A dirty shameful devil of a secret...

Something that two men share. A legacy that will shock you to your very core. One that is created not out of madness, but of the purest desire. Take a vivid journey into the mind of the killer and his biggest fan. Do you believe in evil? See the knife plunge. Lap at the wounds. Do you still? There is no rational meaning or pretty words that will hide away the darkness that the words of this found journal creates. Inside is the real truth. And it can set you free. Watch all you want. Taste what you dare not have.

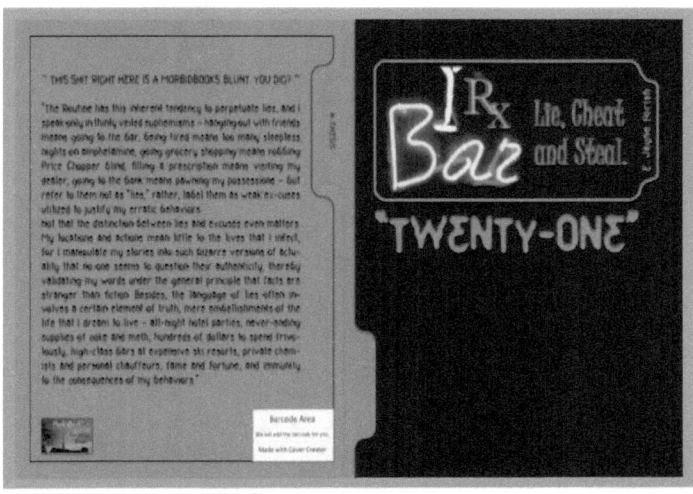

~"The routine has this inherent tendency to perpetuate lies,
and I speak only in thinly veiled euphemisms — hanging out
with friends means going to the bar; being tired means too
many sleepless nights on amphetamine; going grocery
shopping means robbing Price Chopper blind; filling a
prescription means visiting my dealer; going to the bank
means pawning my possessions — but refer to them not as
"lies;" rather, label them as weak excuses utilized to justify my
erratic behaviours.

~I'm feeling down and dirty, feeling kind of mean, so I give those fans my middle finger. Those poor bastards go nuts. My team looks at me in awe. My coach frowns and the opposing one begins to furiously scratch out new plays. I see our opponents and I almost feel sorry for the poor bastards. Their fans can't help them. Their coach can't help them. I'm going to run them off their own track in front of their own fans and there is not one thing they can do about it.

~**Humanity is the devil is a deconstructed nightmare mixing David Lynch and snuff movies.** The plot revolves around a central character, Seth, who is set about a crusade against humanity which, for him, represents pure evil. Through random killings he and his cronies try to accelerate the end of the world, in order to provoke and defeat the Demiurge, the false God that is ruling the earth. As in Burroughs, logical language is replaced here with cut-scenes – sometimes to be taken literally – that plunge the reader into an extreme experience.

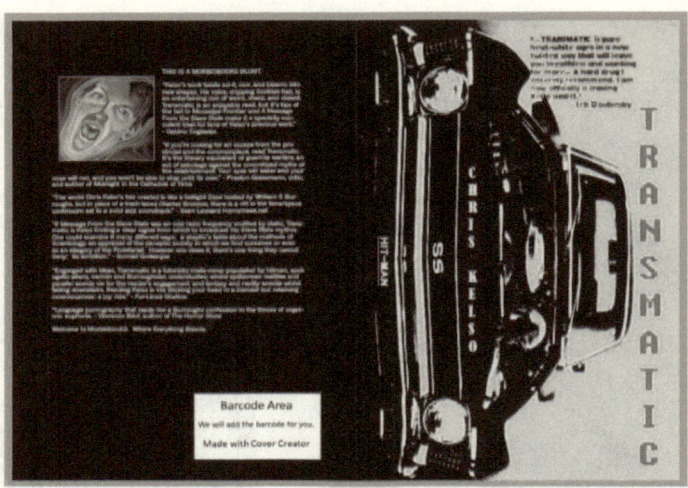

~"As a part-time hitman/exterminator, Ignius Ellis's dream is
to buy a candy-apple red Nova Supreme. In the process of
trying to earn enough cash to make his dream come true he
gets sucked into the rough world of Visitacion Valley, SF.
When the tenants in his apartment complex reveal their
various extracurricular activities this take an even more
bizarre twist and Ellis soon becomes acquainted with the
nightmarish Slave State dimension..."

~That's the last time she gets the bigger worm...

Once their flesh flakes away the angels collapse into puddles
of hissing goop and withered petals blow into them hurried
along by unseen winds. My spit looses its sweet taste to the
black flavor of ash. The glowing birds in the bright orange
sky burst into small sparkly novas. The sky itself weeps and
tears, streaking down like a ruined painting as the dismal
grey of life wheezes back before my eyes. I don't blink;
praying silently for one last desperate sensation of the high.
Lila feels it too. She writhes on the mattress next to me...

~Scary as ever.

He looked at her and grinned wickedly, the overcasting shadows of the outer corner of the stone wall, combined with the flickering light above them, created a deadly feature across the side of his face. He sees her lying helpless. He chuckled eerily, and instantly raised his hand. Her eyes widened to the sight of the gleaming sharp knife in his grasp.

He even held it up for her to see it better.

She stared up at him and then to the knife, panting in fear. Her heart pounded throughout her body as he chuckled once more saying deeply,

"Oh excellent. I've found you . . ."

~**Within these twisted and perverted pages**, Johnson manages to demolish clichés with a jaded finesse that I've personally never encountered in written form. Another apparent talent is his effortless deconstruction of pop-culture allegories and references as found in his story "Vampussy." No one is safe or spared from his dagger sharp sarcasm and wit.

While not without its flaws, my appreciation for this kind of talent and voice is what made his writing so fun to read, even if he might possibly be out of his ever-loving mind.

~In Garrett Cook's Murderland serial killers are idolized by society. Their deeds are followed obsessively by television pundits and the adoring public. A subculture has grown up around this phenomena, called "Reap." Laws are created to allow this activity to flourish, including designated "safe zones' where killers can practice their trade without fear of persecution. Fans of the top rated serial killers celebrate each new kill on social media and television. Programs glorify their deeds.

The culture of Murderland is violent and mirrors our own violent society and its decadent obsessions.

~Born whole from the rectum of a dying patient, Morbid silently stalks the hospital's hallways, heinously dispatching the most helpless of patients and in the most painfully repulsive of manners. In the meantime, in order to pay for his family and home that includes his ghost step-father Sammy and his pet aborted fetus Chip, Westphal has to ingest mounds of dangerous narcotics to get through his night shifts. Barely hanging on to his Care Tech gig by his fingernails, the last thing Westphal needs is to be accused of Morbid's evil deeds. You, on the other hand, simply seek some solace from all Your diseases.

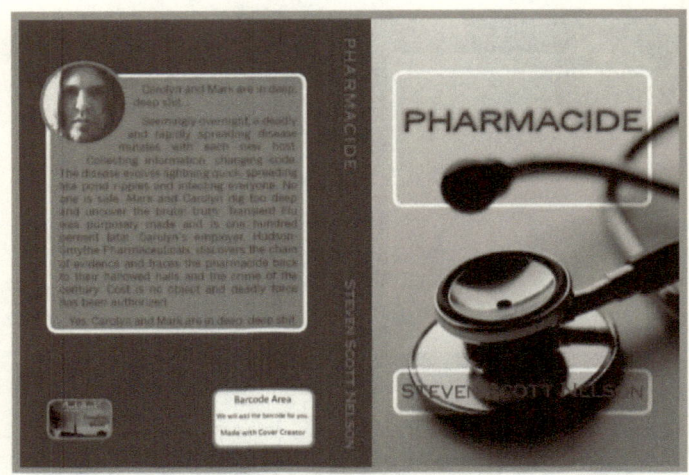

~It looks like Carolyn and Mark are in deep, deep shit...
Mark and Carolyn live in an alternate 1989 where Ronald Reagan is on his fourth presidential term. The USA has a rigid, long-standing caste system and abortions were never made legal. Being homeless is a crime that is punishable by imprisonment in Tent City. Most of Mark's ER patients are inmates at this camp and are victims of a new disease dubbed. Transient Flu. This deadly and rapidly spreading disease mutates with each new host, collecting information, changing code. The disease evolves lightning quick, spreading like pond ripples…

~**IMMANUEL THE CHRIST has some nerve.** Jonah has already lost everyone he loves to Pilate the vampire and his Harbor drug violence. Jonah now trudges through his days staying as high on Plata as possible. He just wants to be left alone while he waits for his turn to die. The Christ has other plans for him. She sends Pedro, to assign Jonah to order the Herod to dismantle the Harbor's Plata trade. Jonah decides to run. But you can't run from God. As Jonah learns the hard way when the 'Edmund Fitzgerald' goes down in rough seas, with the reluctant prophet on board...

~Five Very Wicked Shorts. Brought to you with love and blood from The Grim Reverend Steven Rage, the 'Most Depraved Writer in Print'. ~

Through the sheer shock of his presentation, Rage forces readers to consider the alternatives, to look at the garbage in the streets, to see what is swept into the gutters at night right before all decent people awake to see another cleaned up version of the day. Depravity at its finest, but really the stories are loads of fun.

~Pontius Pilate is cursed to be a vampire. Life after life after life.~ And for the Plata dealing Pilate, his life is more like a death sentence. His only chance surviving is to keep on selling his monthly quota of Plata. This new man-made narcotic is a potent speed-ball designed to amp up the user, while also numbing the conscience into euphoric oblivion. To nullify the pain. To stifle the torture. To run and to hid from all the anguish inside. PILATE is a drug lord vampire in this re-telling of Christ's final days.

~So I, The Spun Monkey, have returned from running my errands, safe and sound. Having failed rehab once again, The Spun Monkey went ahead and procured myself an 8-ball of crispy, crunchy Columbian Bam-Bam. I chipped, chopped, lined and blasted off with two bigguns up each side. OOH OOH EEE EEE-fuckmerunning- OOH-OOH-OOH, motherfuckers! Monkey be ready... Yes, indeeeeeed.... Having had my jet fuel, I then sat my hairy asshole down at the keyboard and began flailing away. The monkey hopes you dig the fruits of my labors in 'The Spun Monkey's Digest'. And if you not ... well then ... you can go eff yourself, Capitan!

~Following religious folklore, parables, and beliefs, Rage presents the readers with a God who truly is the Shepherd that leaves no sheep behind. While this tale is deeply woven with the intricacies of a dark, drug-infested world ruled by evil forces, this is the story of a lost sheep. All are God's children, even the most foulest of evil creatures who by their own will have become so through their spiritual and physical copulation with the Devil, and as such, in God's mercy, still are given a chance to be saved.

~ CARGO CONTAINS:

1. *Space-wrecked on Venus* by NEIL R. JONES
2. *For All the Marbles* by REV. STEVEN RAGE
3. *Tony and the Beetles* by PHILIP K. DICK
4. *Acid Bath* by VASELEOS GARSON
5. *The Butterfly Kiss* by ARTHUR DEKKER SAVAGE
6. *The Moon Destroyers* by MONROE K. RUCH

FROM SOME OF THE GIANTS OF THE GOLDEN AGE to the darkest of dystopian noir, MorbidbookS SciFi Anthology will take you from hopeful space travel to living hand-to-mouth in the despair beneath the Earth.
Welcome to your future.

~**During the height of England's Bubonic Plague an ancient Evil Force strolls into London-Town** in the form of a would-be doctor. It could smell the blood from miles away, wanting only to help. At the hospital where he cares for the victims of this Black Death, the ill come to him unimpeded. They arrived and fell by the scores. With the help of his ever-faithful assistant, Sightless Agnes, a most ravenous cares for them all. Eating his way through an entire hospital, he treats them until there is nothing left. Nothing save their empty eye sockets, a few pounds of leeched bleached bones and some bolts of old dried-out flesh-leather parchment.

~New from MorbidbookS: Where Everything Bleeds is an instant collector's specimen and a certain stunner. ~ Be the first freak on your block to acquire this singular and unexpurgated exquisite culling of The Grim Reverend Steven Rage's favorite 'meds'. Enjoy this one–of–a–kind vivid look into the twisted mind of The Most Depraved Writer In Print as he captains you through the intoxicating stain of his wicked imagination. Included are numerous Photos, Paintings and Illustrations embellished with dramatic grayscale that enhance these iniquitous and magnificent Dark Fantasy fables.

~Click On Image For More MorbidbookS On Kindle~